NEW YORK TIMES BESTSELLING AUTHOR

DONNA ALWARD

Almost a Family

DEDICATION

For my sister Janet, who gave me the kick in the pants to write in the first place, and for her influence on this book.

CHAPTER ONE

Molly Schaeffer stopped the rental car at the end of the snow-drifted driveway. Shoving it into park, she reached inside her purse, searching for the slip of paper with instructions on it, written in her assistant's elegant handwriting. *Next door neighbor number one-thirty-two has Sara and the key to the house. Will expect you Wednesday.*

Well, it was Thursday, but that couldn't be helped, she thought with nervous irritation. She straightened the silk scarf around her neck, then pressed a hand to her trembling stomach. Molly had no control over winter storms and closed airports. Spending the night on a vinyl bench in the Toronto terminal hadn't been her idea of elegant accommodation. She was used to four- and five-star these days.

But getting here had been more important. She checked her reflection in the rearview mirror and tucked a few strands of disobedient hair behind her ears. She took a fortifying breath. As difficult as it had been getting here, it was nothing compared to the job before her.

Putting the rental car into drive again, she inched her way up the snowy lane until she was sitting outside a cute little Cape Cod with blue shutters. Exhausted, she turned off the key and pocketed it, exiting the vehicle in flimsy heels that sank in the packed down snow. Icy cold bits flicked over her feet, so she stamped them against the step as she approached the matching blue door. She hoped this neighbor wouldn't prolong matters. What Molly really wanted was to pick up Sara, put the child to bed for a nap and take a long, steaming bath.

She rang the bell, her fingers shaking from fatigue and nervousness, the beginnings of a headache tensing behind her eyes. She hadn't seen her niece since the girl's first birthday, and now Sara was nearly four. And she'd be staying with Molly for at least the next few weeks, full-time. Molly wasn't sure she was up to the challenge.

The door opened, letting out laughter and ear-splitting squeals and giggles, but her jaw dropped in a most unflattering way when she came face to face with Jason Elliot.

She stared for a long moment. He hadn't changed over the past six years, not really. Though his hair was shorter, it was still thick and black, his eyes still a deep rich brown, the color of espresso. Then there was the hint of dimples, always present, smiling or not. He still filled out his faded jeans like they were tailor-made just for him and his chest was wider, his arms stronger, beneath his tan button-down shirt.

His smile disappeared abruptly. "Molly."

She tried to close her mouth and look composed, but it didn't work. "You? You're the next-door neighbor?"

"Kim didn't tell you?" He frowned, his chocolate brown eyes disapproving.

He looked down her body and she flushed beneath his scrutiny, feeling incredibly stupid as she saw the corners of his lips quirk at the sight of her snowy heels. How was she to know they'd have six inches of new snow today? Who in their right mind wore heavy boots on an *airplane*, anyway?

She tucked her bag under her arms and straightened. "No, she did not. It doesn't matter. I'm here to pick up Sara and take her home."

His gaze met hers and she felt the pull, the one that still tethered them together though years of blame separated them. She swallowed, not wanting to get in any deeper than a basic hello. "Is she ready?"

"You haven't seen her in a long time. Why don't you come in and get acquainted first? We were just about to have a snack."

Well, that plan was foiled. Head high, Molly squeezed by him into the foyer, removing her leather gloves and tucking them into her pockets. He looked good. Too good. Keeping an icy exterior wasn't who she was, but she knew how to do it and donned it like armor. Even after all this time, looking at him made her warm all over. And that was a bad thing.

"We were expecting you yesterday."

Uncomfortable and unsure of how to proceed, she removed her coat and draped it over the newel post of the white banister. "Yes, well, winter hit southern Ontario yesterday, and I was stranded at Pearson. I would have called but I couldn't get through to Kim's hospital room after nine o'clock, because they stop all incoming calls. And I didn't have your number. I'm sorry if it inconvenienced you."

A blonde rocket zoomed into the room. "Uncle Jason, when can I have my cookies, huh?"

Jason bent and picked up the girl, laughing and touching a finger to her nose. "In a minute. Do you remember your Aunt Molly?"

The girl narrowed brown eyes at Molly, deep in thought. "You sent me Barbies for Christmas."

Molly laughed, charmed. "That's right. I hope you liked them."

"Yeah, but Bubbles chewed one's head off."

Molly looked at Jason, confused. "Bubbles?"

"Her dog." He ruffled Sara's hair, his voice and eyes softening. "You go on into the kitchen. We'll have a snack together, then you need to get your things, okay? You're going back to your own house today, muffin."

She took off as quickly as she had arrived, and they stared after her.

"She looks like a handful," Molly remarked, smiling after the tiny bombshell. A handful that was going to be in her charge for the next few weeks. Her smile faltered a little.

"She's energetic and smart, but she's a good kid," Jason defended sharply, and Molly got the feeling that despite the warning note in his tone, Jason wasn't too comfortable with their reunion either. He definitely didn't act *happy* to see her.

"I never meant to imply she wasn't," Molly retorted, avoiding his gaze. *If only this headache would disappear.* She sighed and pressed her fingers to her eyelids.

His voice took on a cool veneer of politeness. "Come on into the kitchen. You look ready to drop. I'll make you some coffee."

She followed him through the living room into the airy kitchen. Sara was already seated in a booster chair at the table, scribbling on paper with crayons. A black and white cat slept in a wicker bed next to the patio doors. While Molly put her purse on the counter, Jason took two chocolate chip cookies out of a blue jar shaped like a cat and poured milk into a sippy cup.

"Here you go, Sara." He put them in front of her, kissed the top of her head and went back to the coffee maker.

"You're very good with her," Molly commented quietly, standing a few feet away and leaning against the gray marble countertop.

"I've lived next door for two years now," he replied, measuring coffee into the filter. "I'm surprised Kim didn't mention it."

Molly's baby sister hadn't mentioned it because she knew that Molly refused to speak of Jason Elliot and their past relationship. Full stop.

"We don't talk about stuff like that much."

That, meaning *them*. His head came up and their gazes met again. They had to quit looking at each other that way, as if they wanted to forget but couldn't help but remember.

"More milk, please."

The sweet voice interrupted them, and Molly was thankful for the diversion. She'd stared at Jason far too long, and he at her. Dredging up the past would do no one any good. "I'll get it," she mumbled and went to the fridge.

Jason poured coffee. "Cream and sugar, right?" he asked, and she hated that he remembered.

"No, black," she answered. She hated it black, but she was going to be here for the better part of a month, and she had to keep things very cool between her and Jason. Dredging up past hurts wouldn't help a thing. The past was the past and it needed to stay that way—making it clear they'd both moved on.

"Didn't you have to work or something today?"

He handed her a mug and a cookie from the jar. "I worked this morning, and did some rearranging of my schedule to be home this afternoon. We had fun, didn't we, Sara?"

"Mmm-hmmm," she answered, her mouth full of chocolate crumbs. She swallowed. "I fed the kitties. Then we made hot dogs and cookies. I only like ketchup."

Molly could only assume the ketchup was meant for the hotdogs and not for the cookies. She swallowed. "Kitties and hotdogs and cookies, oh my. My work is cut out for me."

Jason raised an eyebrow at her tight tone. "I took her into the clinic with me. I've taken quite a bit of time off since last week, though, and the other vet is getting tired of covering for me. I'm glad you're here." He looked out the window, away from her.

Like hell, Molly thought, but she pasted on a smile and sipped the bitter coffee, missing her cream and sugar.

"Kim's doing okay? I only talked to her the once, after she came out of surgery and asked if I could come. I should go in this afternoon, but I'm afraid I need a bath and a nap before I go anywhere." She hated to ask any advice about Sara, but without Kim's input, Jason was the only one who had an idea of the little girl's schedule. "Does Sara nap in the afternoon?"

"Sometimes, but only if you get her tired enough first. She's had a busy day so far. You might get lucky."

Getting lucky. Molly sniffed. It had been so long since Molly had "gotten lucky" that she hardly remembered it. Her life in Calgary didn't facilitate many personal relationships. But with Jason mere steps away, she couldn't help remembering being with him. Remember what it was like to touch—and be touched—by him. And she knew it was time she and Sara got a move on.

"We should go. Does she have a bag or anything?"

"I'll get it." He left the room, leaving her alone with her niece for the first time.

Molly approached the tot and put on her friendliest smile. "Hey, you. We're gonna head back to your house, okay? Jason's just getting your bag, and we can take the car I rented. Then you can show me your room and all your toys."

"No, thanks. I like it here." Sara's tiny fingers grasped a red crayon and she began drawing circles, unconcerned.

Molly sighed. Why couldn't this be easy? She was unsure how to proceed, having so little experience with children. Fact was, she'd spent very little time in the company of *any* children.

"Well, Jason does have a nice house, doesn't he?" She smiled down at the girl with what she hoped looked like an encouraging invitation. "But won't you like being in your own bed tonight? I bet you have a pink room, right? And a favorite stuffed animal to sleep with. I know I did when I was a little girl."

Sara's gaze darted up suspiciously. "What was his name?"

Molly's face relaxed, glad Sara had taken the bait. "It was a she. A fluffy brown teddy bear named Honey. I still have her in my apartment back in Calgary."

The crayon forgotten, Sara squirmed in her booster seat. "Really?"

"Yup. Look, Sara, I know we don't know each other very well, but your mom asked me to come take care of you while she's in the hospital. And then we can get to know each other a lot better, okay? We'll have lots of fun, you'll see." She wasn't sure who she was trying to convince more—Sara or herself.

"Will you take me to see Mommy?"

Jason came back in carrying a pink backpack and Molly blushed, looking to him for help.

"Listen, sweet thing," he said gently, coming over to the table and kneeling beside her. "You know your mom's in the hospital, and she had an operation. She's still pretty sick."

At the girl's crestfallen face, he sighed. "I'll tell you what. I'll talk to Molly and your mom tomorrow, and, if it's okay, I'll take you both to the hospital after work. How's that sound?"

Sara's eyes glistened and Molly's heart broke. Whatever the inconvenience to her schedule, whatever issues she had with Jason, they simply weren't as important as what this little girl was going through. Sara's whole world revolved around her mother. Now she hadn't seen her mother in nearly a week, and she had to be afraid, insecure. How much did she actually understand? Something told Molly that Jason had turned his life upside down during that time to make things okay for Sara. The least she could do was help him out.

"Hey, Sara?" Molly ran a finger under Sara's eye, gently wiping away a tear. "I'll make you a deal. You and I go home and have a rest. It's been a busy day!" She smiled brightly. "And then, after we eat dinner, maybe we can call your mom on the phone and you can talk to her. Does that sound like a plan?"

Sara nodded, and Molly's answering grin was triumphant. At least she'd done something right.

They bundled Sara in her heavy jacket and mittens, and Molly took the backpack. "Okay, we're off!"

"Um, Molly, hang on a sec. You need the car seat out of my truck. I'll put it in for you."

Jason slipped on a pair of utterly practical winter boots and a jacket, and to Molly's dismay, it made him appear even more rugged and manly.

"I can do it myself." Her voice came out more churlish than she intended.

He aimed a mocking glance at her footwear. "Whatever."

He slid past her and jogged to his sport utility while she fumed in the background, shoving on her gloves and fishing for her keys.

It was her job to look after Sara, and she'd do it well. She didn't need any help from Jason Elliot. Nope, she didn't need him at all. She'd done just fine without him, and she'd continue to do so.

Two hours later she was recanting that thought.

Sara had slept for precisely half an hour. Just long enough for Molly to have half a bath. Hearing the little girl up and about, Molly groggily drained the water and pulled on Kim's bathrobe.

"That's Mommy's!" Sara accused belligerently, her cheeks hot.

Then Molly spent the next twenty minutes reassuring Sara that she had only borrowed the robe for a few moments.

After changing into jeans and a sweater, she turned on the television and let Sara watch cartoons while she searched for food. Kim's house was drastically different from Molly's. Molly had a one-bedroom condo downtown. It was carefully and expensively decorated, completely appropriate for a single working woman. The fridge was only ever half full, and she ate a lot of frozen foods with the word "gourmet" on the label. Kim's house, on the other hand, was littered with toys, the furniture comfortable and well broken in, the table and chairs slightly scarred. One thing Kim did have, however, was a deep freeze and a pantry. Unfortunately, not much was in them beyond baking goods. Did the woman make everything from scratch? Molly's idea of baked goods were what she bought at the corner bakery on the way home from work.

The perishables in the fridge were past the point of no return, and Molly dumped most of them in the garbage. Searching the freezer, she found a small box of chicken nuggets and a bag of French fries. Ah, finally. Convenience food.

"Hey, Sara, how's chicken nuggets sound for supper?"

No answer.

"Sara?"

Still no answer.

Molly dropped the frozen food in the sink and ran to the living room. The television was on, but Sara wasn't there.

She took the stairs two at a time and slid to a halt before the bathroom.

There, on a stepstool, was Sara, happily smearing red lipstick on her face.

Molly took a deep breath. "Sara? What are you doing?"

"Looking pretty!" She aimed a happy smile at her aunt.

"Where did you get the lipstick?" Molly took a slow step into the bathroom, and Sara's smile faded.

"From your bag."

"Did I say you could go into my things?"

"No." The little voice was hardly audible and she stared at her toes. Molly saw the bottom red lip start to tremble and she tried to remember to be patient. Sara was only a child and the accident had thrown her routine completely out the window. She took the tube of twenty-dollar tinting, capped it and put it back in her make-up bag.

Molly grabbed a Kleenex from the box on the counter and tilted up the girl's head. "So next time you're going to ask, right?"

The chin bobbed up and down quickly.

"Okay. Let's get this cleaned up a bit. I found some chicken nuggets for supper. Maybe you can help me make them. And after supper you'll have a bath and we'll call your mom."

"Okay, Aunt Molly." The tiny voice was innocently acquiescent now.

Molly wiped the garish color from Sara's lips.

"Aunt Molly?"

"Hmm?"

"Can Uncle Jason come over? I miss him."

Me too.

The thought came so quickly, Molly had no chance to guard against it. Where in the world had that come from? She hadn't seen Jason in six years. Not since she'd left for law school. Not since he'd left to become a veterinarian. And if she thought of him now and then, big deal! It didn't necessarily mean anything. It didn't mean she *missed* him.

You didn't forget your first love. Or your first broken heart.

"Not tonight, okay? Hey, where's Bubbles? I thought you had a dog."

"Uncle Jason's dog-sitting." Sara grinned. "I'm gonna be a dog-sitter when I grow up."

Molly ran a hand through her still damp hair. Jason was everywhere. Molly had no idea how to look after a preschool-aged child. Meanwhile, she had a dozen files in her briefcase that needed attention.

It was going to be a very long three weeks.

Jason poured another cup of coffee, went to the cupboard and took out the whiskey bottle. Staring out the window over the sink, he spun off the cap and made his coffee Irish.

Molly.

He'd known for four days that she was coming. He'd had four days to prepare himself for her arrival, but it hadn't been enough.

He took a long, punishing drink of caffeine and liquor. She hadn't changed. Except maybe she was more beautiful now than before. She'd pinned her blonde hair into a snooty sweep, but he'd seen the tendrils tucked behind her ears and remembered taking pins from her hair years past, how the long tresses had fallen over his hands, through his fingers like silk. Her eyes, once innocent and trusting, were now older and more guarded, but no less intriguing. Her lips were full and had been carefully tinted with red lipstick. She'd waltzed in here in her designer shoes and her expensive coat that probably had cost more than his living room furniture, and had figured she'd take over. That much was plain.

She'd always thought she'd known everything. He scowled. She always had to be right. Even all those years ago, when he'd begged her to stay, she'd turned a deaf ear. Seeing her today should have been nothing.

Nothing. Instead he'd opened the door and had felt like he'd been sucker-punched in the gut.

Jason shook his head and drained his cup. *That* sort of thinking wasn't going to help anything. The house seemed quieter without Sara already. He wondered how Molly was making out with her. Bedtime was the hardest part of the day for Sara. It was the time when Kim read Sara her favorite story and sang lullabies. Jason had tried his best and they'd managed, but Molly didn't know the child at all. She had no idea how to look after a toddler. She didn't know potty emergencies or nightmares or grapes cut in half. She knew files and legal documents and corporations.

The focus had to be on Sara. He put his empty mug in the sink and grabbed his jacket off of the back of a kitchen chair. If he had to see Molly at the same time, well, it couldn't be helped. That was *not* why he was going, he assured himself.

He rang the bell twice. When his finger was poised to ring the third time, Molly opened the door, her neat sweep of hair now in shambles, her face devoid of makeup, her sleeves pushed to the elbows and water splashed all over the front of her pink sweater.

"What in the blue blazes are you doing?" Jason pushed his way inside.

Molly shut the door behind him and he heard her sigh with frustration. "Bath time. You could have warned me, you know."

He chuckled. "Sara loves bath time. Did you find her squirty shark?"

"Find it? I'm wearing it." Her voice was clipped and annoyed. She went past him and headed up the stairs again. "I shouldn't leave her up there alone. Excuse me."

When she was gone, Jason wandered into the kitchen, catching his breath at the sight he found. Kim's normally ordered kitchen was a disaster. For two people, they'd made an extraordinary mess. Plates smeared with ketchup, glasses with the scum of chocolate milk in the bottom and a greasy cookie sheet were piled in the sink. A thick blob of ketchup was on the tablecloth and a dishtowel stained brown was crumpled on the counter where it had wiped up a spill.

He shook his head. Molly had come home to take care of things, but it was obvious she was out of her depth. He opened the dishwasher and began loading the plates and glasses inside.

"What do you think you're doing?"

He turned to find Molly, her arms full of a scrubbed and shiny Sara, leveling an accusing glare at him.

"Just loading your dishwasher."

"I can do that. I *do* know how."

He floundered, straightened. "I know that."

Molly put Sara down, resting a hand on the child's damp curls. "What exactly are you doing here, Jason?"

He stared at Molly for a few seconds, then knelt down, putting on a brilliant smile for Sara. "I came to say goodnight to my best girl. The house seemed kinda quiet tonight."

He held out his arms and Sara rushed into them, smelling of baby shampoo and lotion and clean pajamas.

He laughed. "Here." He nuzzled her neck, making her giggle. "Bubbles sent a kiss goodnight."

Sara gripped Jason's face, stuck out her tongue and swiped a puppy kiss right up his cheek.

"Sara!" Molly's voice intruded, appalled, as Jason wiped the slobber from his face. Molly took a step forward, her mouth pursed in dismay.

Jason stopped Molly's progress with a look. "I think that was meant for Bubbles. But you know the rules about Snoopy kisses, muffin." Jason looked Sara evenly in the eye as she nodded back at him, chastised.

"No Snoopy kisses. They're yucky."

"That's right. Time for bed now."

She peeked at him over Molly's shoulder as they disappeared, and Jason ran a hand through his hair. Bedtime wasn't going to be that bad, it seemed. Sara wasn't making a big fuss about it at all. He should go home now while Molly was upstairs.

Yet something held him back, made him stay. Maybe it was the way Molly's eyes darkened with doubt just before she shuttered them away. Maybe it was six years of wondering what had happened to her. Maybe it was nothing other than simple curiosity about whether her life had turned out the way she had wanted.

Whatever it was, it kept him there and he went to the living room to wait for her return.

CHAPTER TWO

After reading her a story and singing three songs, Molly finally had Sara asleep. All the frustration Molly had felt throughout the day evaporated as she'd looked down on Sara's sleeping face. Innocent and trusting. With her blonde curls and long eyelashes, she looked like a slumbering angel. Kim had been raising this little spitfire all on her own, and Molly had a new appreciation for the courage and commitment it took to be a parent. Not to mention a single one.

The hall was quiet, and she assumed Jason had gone as she quietly descended the stairs. *He didn't even wait to say goodbye*, she thought, feeling a little let down and a little relieved at the same time. It was probably just as well. Seeing him was hard enough. It brought back all the memories of their breakup, and worse, the memories of when times had been good. And it had been good—for a long time. But that was over. It would be better for everyone if they tried to keep out of each other's way over the next few weeks.

Wandering to the kitchen, she sighed. Having kids required sacrifices. Sacrifices she was positive she wasn't ready to make. In that she was sure she'd made the right choice. She had too many things to do before she thought about having children of her own. She remembered the way Jason had kissed Sara's head as he'd given her milk that afternoon. No, she was where she wanted to be. No matter how the sight of Jason and Sara together twisted her insides.

She was in the middle of pouring water into the electric kettle when Jason spoke behind her.

"You making tea?"

She spun, splashing water on the counter. "I thought you'd gone."

"I probably should have."

Her body shook, not from the surprise but because he was here, in the flesh, and she'd been thinking about him. His posture was relaxed, but everything about him made her pay attention. Right now it was the dimple crawling up his cheek that distracted her.

Molly turned back and shut off the tap. "I'm extremely tired," she explained stiffly. "Sara only slept half an hour today and I didn't sleep very well stranded at the airport last night."

"You actually slept in the airport?"

"We were only delayed, not cancelled. Except the delay ended up being most of the night. I didn't take the hotel voucher. I was afraid I'd miss the next flight and I wanted to get here as soon as I could." She plugged in the kettle and searched for a mug and the tea bags, deliberately taking out only one. "Whatever you stayed to say, I'd rather get into it another time."

She dropped the tea bag into a mug and faced him. He was staring at her steadily, his expression unreadable.

"What are you thinking?" The words came out slightly breathless, and she grimaced inwardly.

"I'm thinking about how beautiful you still are. I can't believe I'd forgotten." He shoved his hands in his pockets and leaned against the doorway to the kitchen.

Her heart beat erratically as a memory slid in, unwanted. Their first kiss, on prom night. They'd been slow dancing, and he'd curled a hand around her neck and whispered, "You are so beautiful." Even then, at the innocent age of seventeen, the smoothness of his voice had been able to raise all the fine hairs on her body. When he'd leaned in to touch his lips to hers, meeting them had been the most natural thing in the world.

She stiffened, defending herself against memories. "It's been six years, Jason. I'm here for exactly three weeks. That's all."

"So I hear. Why did you agree to come exactly, Molly?"

She unplugged the kettle as it began to scream. "Because Kim asked me. Because she's my only sister and she needs me."

"Molly to the rescue, is that it?"

Pouring the water and ignoring the bitterness in his voice, she replied, "Nothing of the kind. I had some holidays coming to me, and I brought work with me. There's no reason I can't do both."

Jason laughed sharply, then boosted himself away from the door with a shoulder and took another mug out of the cupboard.

"What's so funny?" Molly dipped out her tea bag, added milk and took a sip as she noticed he knew exactly where to find things in Kim's kitchen.

"You thinking you can work and keep an eye on Sara. Believe me, it's not as easy as you think."

"You did it. Just this morning, in fact."

He eyed her shrewdly. "Yes, I did. And it wasn't easy, juggling animals and clients and kids for five hours. Thankfully, my staff likes Sara as much as I do. We've all been making do and helping out."

He made it sound as if he were such a paragon of virtue. She'd never met anyone who could make her feel as small and incapable as Jason Elliot. She took her cup and walked away, heading for the living room before she said something snotty and rude. Why couldn't he just leave so she could get some sleep? She was sure she wouldn't be so crabby if she could get seven or eight hours of uninterrupted rest.

He followed her, to her supreme annoyance.

"Sara's favorite breakfast foods are toast with peanut butter and apple juice or toaster waffles and syrup. But she doesn't like any butter on them, just the syrup."

"I'm sure we'll manage just fine."

"She's potty trained, so you'll be okay there."

"Jason, stop it." Molly put her cup on an end table and clenched her fists. "I can handle it. Sara can actually speak for herself, quite well for a girl her age, I think. I'm twenty-seven years old and have been looking after myself for some time now. I don't need you to ride in on your white horse and save the day, got it? You're free to get back to your practice. You've made sure we're settled. Your duty to us is hereby discharged."

She cringed at her shrewish tone. She didn't want to pick a fight or stir up recriminations. What was it about him that got under her skin?

"You really haven't changed, have you?" Jason put down his own cup and squared off against her. He was only inches away, close enough she could smell his cologne. He flexed his fingers, snapping the index ones with his thumbs. "You always had to do everything yourself. Had to *prove* yourself. Do everything your way, with no help from anyone."

"You know why," she answered in a low, threatening voice. Their gazes locked and hers warned him not to dig too deep into the past. He knew the secrets she held inside, the ones that brought out that need for independence and her eyes begged him not to use them against her now.

He snorted with derision but backed off just a little. "I thought that after all these years, you'd be over it. I should have known."

"And I would have thought that you'd have learned you can't control other people's lives and have everything your way. But I guess you haven't changed either," she retorted without thinking. She pressed a hand to her forehead, annoyed that she'd been goaded into responding. Six hours. Less than six hours home and they were arguing already.

"So where does that leave us?" Agitated, he ran his hands through his hair, his eyes openly hostile.

She smiled thinly. "Exactly where we were before today. You have your life. I have mine. Let's keep it that way."

"Fine," he bit out, glaring. "You'll be begging for my help before the week is out."

He stomped to the door and she heard it slam behind him. "The hell I will," she muttered to herself.

Molly was exhausted by the time Jason picked them up to go to the hospital the following evening. She'd broached the subject of going without him to Sara and had met with stiff resistance. The child was clearly attached to her "Uncle" Jason, and rather than rock the boat, Molly acquiesced. How one child could demand so much attention, she wasn't sure. But she knew that keeping the house in order and entertaining Sara had filled her day, leaving her no time to even open her briefcase.

The dinner mess was at least tidied up when he arrived. He looked big and outdoorsy-handsome in his thick brown coat and heavy boots. His hair had been whipped up by the winter wind, his cheeks were ruddy with cold. She opened the door, left it ajar and went to get her own coat, leaving him standing silently in the gap while the brisk air rushed into the foyer.

"Come on, Sara. It's time to go."

Sara came around the corner carrying a teddy bear and a folded piece of paper. Molly fluffed her hair over the collar of her coat and knelt to help Sara put on her winter boots.

They still hadn't spoken, and it was getting on Molly's nerves—feeling his big presence behind her, knowing he was standing there. Close enough to touch. Close enough to be folded into those strong arms, enveloped in his jacket. How she could want to and still feel so hostile toward him confused her.

"Why don't you drive my rental?" she suggested, stuffing Sara's arms into her jacket. "That way we don't have to move the seat back and forth."

"Fine," he said quietly. She could feel the heat from his body as he leaned inside further, reaching to pick up the keys from the small table by her left hip. Her heart beat just a little bit faster at the his nearness.

"Okay!" she said brightly to Sara while her insides trembled. It wasn't only Jason. She was going to see Kim, too, and was afraid of what she might see, how she might feel seeing her sister lying broken in a hospital bed. She hadn't seen Kim in a couple of years. This wasn't exactly how she'd envisioned their next meeting.

"We're all ready. Got your card?"

Sara held up her folded paper in a fuzzy mitten.

"I've got my purse. Let's go."

She locked the door behind them, leaving on the porch light. The sedan was already warming up, and Jason came forward to scoop up Sara and secure her in her seat. Head held high, Molly opened the passenger door herself and got inside, buckling her seat belt.

He pulled out of the drive, everyone eerily quiet.

She glanced over at his legs. He was in jeans again, faded ones that creased at the knee as he sat. His jaw held a hint of dark stubble, and his fingers—those long, glorious fingers—were gripping the steering wheel, encased in brown leather gloves that matched his coat.

Fingers that had touched her intimately years before. Fingers that had wiped her tears and had fed her chocolates at Christmas. Fingers that he'd once loved to sink into her hair...ones that had touched her skin...

Scowling, she turned her head and stared out the window at the inky darkness of the river as they headed into Fredericton. Ten minutes. In ten minutes, they'd be at the hospital and out of this silent prison. In ten minutes, she could stop smelling him and feeling him so close.

"Uncle Jason?"

"Yes, sweetie?"

"Are you mad at Aunt Molly?"

Before she could stop it, Molly's head swiveled in his direction and his gaze met hers. She felt her heart leap at the emotion there. It wasn't animosity. It was acceptance. Acceptance of the inevitability of how things were between them. She wondered if her eyes mirrored the same thoughts. That the things they hadn't resolved six years ago still hung between them.

He looked in the rearview mirror as he answered the child. "No, Sara. I'm not mad at your Aunt Molly."

"Then why aren't you talking?"

Molly hid a smile and waited for his answer.

"Aw, we're just thinking about seeing your mommy again. I know she's excited to see you."

Molly's lips curved deeper at his clear manipulation, turning the topic away from them.

"I made her a card."

"I see that. She'll love it. I know she misses you. But she still has an owie, okay? You'll have to be very careful getting up on her bed and stuff."

"I know."

Molly stared out the window again, wondering about the thought process of a three-year-old. What did Sara think and understand about what had happened to her mother? Did she even grasp the enormity of the accident? Cracked ribs and a ruptured spleen were nothing to fool with, and neither was a concussion. It had been the better part of a week and this was the first time Kim had been alert enough to see her own daughter. Molly didn't even know exactly what had happened. All Kim had been able to manage through the medications was a brief phone call asking for help. The weak, thready voice on the line had frightened Molly sufficiently. She'd started making arrangements as soon as her hands had stopped shaking. She had meant to ask as soon as she arrived, but seeing Jason had made her so uncomfortable that she'd tried to keep their conversations to a minimum.

Now her sister was well enough for them to visit, and Molly was glad Kim was recovering nicely despite the seriousness of her injuries. She hadn't hesitated to come and help, but she only had three weeks off and then she had to be back to work. She thought back to the files she'd brought with her. Land leases and royalty contracts. Even on vacation, she couldn't afford to slack off a bit. A week after her scheduled return, she'd have her performance review and she'd know if she got her promotion. A promotion that would entitle her to a corner office with her own paralegal and a raise—not to mention a lovely stock option.

She smiled to herself. She never would have had the same opportunity had she stayed in New Brunswick. Moving to Calgary and getting into the corporate legal business had been her smartest move. And she'd never regretted her decision. Much.

Jason pulled into the hospital parking lot, went down the second row and found a space.

"Okay, munchkin. Let's go see your mama."

He carried Sara inside and went straight to the information desk, Molly trailing behind.

"I'm looking for Kim Shaeffer's room number, please."

The woman behind the desk peered at her computer screen over her glasses, then looked up owlishly. "Who is visiting?"

He smiled his most charming smile, eyes twinkling. "Her daughter and her sister."

The woman wasn't fooled. "And you are?"

Without missing a beat, he winked at the woman and answered, "Her husband."

Molly saw the woman's lips twitch slightly before she handed him a slip of paper and shooed him on his way.

They crowded into the elevator. Molly knit her brows together and hissed, "That was shameful."

Jason shrugged, unconcerned as he hit the button for the proper floor. "It's immediate family only. It's no big deal."

Molly stiffened her spine. It shouldn't bother her that Jason Elliot got a kick out of pretending to be her sister's husband. It shouldn't matter that he could still turn on the charm and women simpered. But it did, and she was severely annoyed with herself for letting it affect her. He'd probably done it simply to antagonize her, she thought, and shoved her hands into her coat pockets. After tonight, she was going to avoid him every chance she got. She was here to look after Sara and Kim. That was it. She wasn't here to take nauseating walks down memory lane with Jason. What would be the point?

The doors slid open and she looked up at Sara, happily ensconced in Jason's arms, clutching her handmade card in pink mittens. It was a fetching picture, her blondeness next to his dark looks. They stepped out, and Jason led the way to the proper ward.

It smelled like hospital—sickness and antiseptic and yesterday's meatloaf. All hushed voices and white scrubbed floors and stainless steel.

He checked his paper, then continued down a hallway until he stopped in front of a half-opened white door.

His eyes lost their flippancy as he suggested quietly to Molly, "Why don't you go in first and make sure it's okay?"

She nodded and took a step into the room, her heart beating quickly in her chest.

"Hey," she said softly and smiled a little at the sight of her sister lying silently in the bed.

Kim was wearing a blue hospital gown and an IV was connected to her arm. But her color was much better than Molly had expected.

"Hey, yourself." Kim attempted a smile, but the bruise on her left cheek held her back, making it more of a grimace. She touched her limp blonde hair with her free hand. "I look a mess. Where's Sara?"

Molly perched carefully on the edge of the bed. "Outside with Jason. God, sis, you look horrible." She grinned, but it didn't cover the worry she felt as she looked down at her sister. "I brought the five-minute repair kit. Are you up to it?"

"*Please*," Kim said, and, with a gasp, pushed herself up to a semi-sitting position. Molly rose, went to the end of the bed and pushed a button to change the angle so Kim was sitting more comfortably.

She pulled a small bag out of her purse. With quick, deft strokes, she brushed out her sister's hair and pulled it up in a perky, cute ponytail. "Why didn't you tell me Jason was the next door neighbor?"

She said it casually, but there was steel was beneath the question and she knew Kim heard it.

"Would you have come?"

Molly adjusted the elastic, frowned and pulled it out to begin again. "I don't know."

Kim held still while Molly pulled her hair up again. "I needed you to come. I knew if you knew Jason was involved, you wouldn't." They kept their voices hushed, knowing he was just outside the door.

"You haven't mentioned it in two years. That's how long he's lived there, right?" She gave a final tug on Kim's hair. "There. That's the best I can do."

"It hasn't been washed since the surgery," Kim lamented. "I'd kill for a bottle of shampoo and conditioner."

Molly took out make up and began putting foundation on a white wedge-shaped sponge.

"You don't talk about Jason. I know that. So I never mentioned him. But as you have probably guessed, he's a godsend to Sara and me."

Hmmph, Molly groused to herself. Almighty Jason the great savior. Perfect Jason, while self-centered Molly was the one to run away. If only people had heard her side of things. But she'd left town, making that her fault, she supposed. And Kim had a point. Jason was the one topic she avoided at all costs. Even if Kim *had* tried to mention it, Molly would have shut her down.

"We'll discuss it later. Now hold still." She made the words gentle, knowing it wasn't Kim's fault she was defensive about Jason. She finished dotting on the sheer foundation, added a hint of mascara, a touch of blush to give her sister a little healthy color and a swipe of lip gloss.

"Now you look presentable. Except for your clothes, but there's nothing I can do there. Can I get Jason and Sara now?"

Kim nodded. "Thanks, Mol. I didn't want to scare her."

Molly stepped outside the door, smiled and took Sara from Jason's arms. "Let's go. Your mama's waiting," she said lightly and carried the little girl inside with Jason on her heels.

"Mommy!"

Sara squirmed with delight at the sight of her mother, and Molly's eyes stung sharply at the unadulterated love in that one word. "Remember, you've got to be careful, Sara. Just sit on her bed easy, okay? Your mom's still pretty sore."

"How's my best girl?" Kim held out her arm to her daughter, wincing slightly but beaming as Sara snuggled in for a big hug. "Gosh, I missed you!"

"I missed you, too. Aunt Molly helped me make you this." Her tiny hands held out the card.

"Wow! You did a great job! Maybe Uncle Jason can put it on my windowsill with my other cards. Is that okay?"

Molly perched at the foot of the bed while Jason took the chair beside it.

"Have you been good for Aunt Molly and Uncle Jason?"

Molly got a strange surge of feeling hearing their names paired together like that. It made them sound like a couple, and if they'd been married years ago like Jason had wanted, it would be true. She kept her eyes from finding his. Long looks were just another thing she had to avoid.

Sara nodded enthusiastically.

"If I asked them, would they say you've been good?"

Jason chuckled. "She's an angel."

Molly touched Sara's hair. "Remember, we can't stay long. Your mama's still pretty tired."

"I remember, Aunt Molly."

Kim hugged her daughter close, careful of her tubes. Jason stood, hovering by the bed. "Have you eaten dinner?"

Kim smiled wryly. "Some chicken and cold mashed potatoes. Gotta love hospital food."

"Do you want something? Molly and I can go to the cafeteria before it closes and grab you a snack."

"I'd love a hot chocolate and a chocolate chip cookie, if you think you can sneak it in."

He nodded and led Molly outside. "I thought they could use some time alone."

"I agree." The fact that they happened to agree on anything seemed some sort of progress. They headed to the elevator and waited for a down arrow. Except time alone for Molly and Sara meant time alone for them, too. Molly struggled to keep things light. "Did you have dinner yet?"

"No. I didn't finish at the clinic until ten minutes before I picked you up."

"I'm sorry."

He looked sideways at her. "Don't be. It's not your fault. I'll grab something at home later."

Silence fell and Molly wished the elevator would hurry. Things were awkward now, no matter how hard she tried for it to be otherwise. Being around Jason was incredibly difficult, because simply looking at him was a reminder of all they'd shared. And of all they'd thrown away. Staying neutral around each other, with all that history pushing at Molly's memory, made it impossible to think of him as only an old friend. They'd shared too much.

"Molly?"

Jason was holding the elevator, and she blushed. "Sorry." She stepped inside and turned while the doors slid shut, keeping them in a square cocoon of intimacy.

Oh, wasn't this grand? She could smell him, the same scent he'd worn since forever. Her heart pounded foolishly. There'd been a time when they would have taken the opportunity to steal a kiss in an elevator; now they stayed on their respective sides and tried fruitlessly to pretend the other wasn't there.

After what seemed like forever, the elevator stopped and they walked to the cafeteria. Wordlessly, Jason got two hot chocolates, a bag of chocolate chip cookies and poured himself a coffee.

Molly took a large Styrofoam cup and poured her own coffee. Then at the cashier, she put her hand on Jason's arm, a silent offer to pay.

"I'll get it," he said.

He handed the woman at the register a twenty-dollar bill.

"Thank you," Molly murmured, trying not to feel beholden.

"Forget it."

His voice was low and husky and Molly felt shivers erupt on her skin. She and Jason were over. They had been for a long time. He infuriated her and she wished he'd simply disappear for the next few weeks so she could look after her sister and niece without interference. She wanted that almost as much as she wanted to know if he still tasted the same. If his arms still felt as strong and sure around her. If it still were possible to lose herself in his delicious brown eyes.

They found a table in the corner next to several boxes of Christmas decorations that had been taken down but not put back into storage. Molly blew on her coffee and braved a look up.

"Kim couldn't tell me much about what happened," she explained quietly. "How much do you know?"

Jason took a deep breath, his dark eyes clouding over with pain. He toyed with his coffee cup. "She was coming home from work, driving the old highway. It was snowing and you know how slippery it gets.... She tried to stop. A man was coming through the light and couldn't get stopped for the red. Kim had the right of way, but it was too slick. She saw him, but lost control coming into the intersection and he hit her, then spun off and took out a pole. Car's totaled." He took a breath. "They rushed her into surgery. The ER was busy, apparently. There were over forty accidents that day."

Molly's face blanched. "My God."

Jason swallowed. "Someone called nine-one-one. I was listed as her emergency contact. By the time I got here, they'd already taken her into the OR."

Molly pushed away the coffee. She should be horrified at what Kim had been through, but for some odd reason, she was stuck on the fact that her ex-boyfriend was her sister's "in case of emergency" number, and that she, as Kim's only family, wasn't listed. Sure, it was far more practical for it to be Jason, as Kim's next-door neighbor. Yet the knowledge, the *exclusion*, still stung.

"What happened to the other driver?"

Jason pushed back his chair, his expression clearly closed. "He died."

Molly's stomach dropped as the seriousness of the accident sunk in. Her only family could have been gone in an instant. The man who had died—surely he had a family who now missed him terribly. It easily could have been Kim. With that quick realization came the knowledge that she had done her sister a terrible disservice by distancing herself.

"Thank you for telling me," she murmured. "I didn't know how to ask Kim...didn't want to upset her. Does she know about the other driver?"

The pain she saw in his dark eyes answered her question, even as he nodded. "She knows. The look on her face when she found out is one I'll never forget."

Molly stared up at him. It was becoming increasingly clear Jason had deep, genuine feelings for her sister. Molly had no right to be jealous of the intimate nature of their relationship, but she felt it all the same. It made no sense for her to resent their closeness. She'd left Jason years ago, and he was free to be close to whomever he chose. But she did resent it. Maybe if she'd been a better sister, Kim would have needed him less.

When they returned to Kim's room, Kim was snuggled up with her daughter, who was on the verge of drifting off to sleep.

Molly put the sack of cookies on the table and smiled gently, more conscious than ever of how precarious life could be. Sara needed her mother. If Kim had been the one killed... Molly's smile wobbled.

She would have lost a sister. Sara would have lost a mother, and then who would she have had?

"She misses you."

Kim smiled back, a perfect beam of maternal love. "I miss her. I'm going crazy in here."

Jason put down his cardboard tray of cups. "Any news on when we can spring you?" he inquired softly.

She shook her head. "It's still too soon. My ribs need more time, and I've had major abdominal surgery. There's no way I could look after Sara myself."

Her eyes moistened and her bottom lip quivered. "Thank you, both of you. I know it's such an imposition..."

"Don't be silly. Where else would I be?" Molly chided softly.

"In Calgary, doing your job." Kim sniffed away her tears. "I know how important it is to you."

Molly shrugged, wishing her sister hadn't felt it necessary to point out the importance of her career in front of Jason. "*You're* important to me."

Sara's eyes opened fully and she sat up. Jason grinned and gave her a cookie from the sack and a sip of the cooling hot chocolate. "We'd better get going," he suggested. "You've got some contraband here and then you need some sleep. We'll come back soon."

Molly chuckled. "I don't think we're going to be able to keep Sara away now."

She rose while Jason shoved Sara's arms into her jacket. "Say bye to Mom," he told her, and she did, giving Kim a huge kiss, and then snuggled into Jason's shoulder. Molly winked at Kim as they left.

It wasn't until they were crossing the parking lot that Molly felt Jason's hand at the small of her back, the gentle pressure making the skin beneath her coat tingle. She looked up at Sara; she was sleeping already, her face nestled against Jason's neck, lips dropped open in fatigue.

He'd be a wonderful father, she thought as she stared up at him. He'd always wanted to be one, and she wondered why he wasn't by now. He had so much going for him—he was breathtakingly handsome, had a successful business, wanted a family. What woman wouldn't want him?

Except her, obviously. She hadn't been ready for a family and hadn't been willing to give up her dreams for his. Now she had everything she wanted in her life in Calgary. Right.

They reached the car and she waited while he gently tucked a sleeping Sara into her seat. He came to open her door and reached around her body to put the key in the lock, his bulk pressing against her back. For a moment, just a moment, she let herself lean back against his weight, the frosty clouds of their breath mingling together in the air. She heard him swallow close to her ear, was dimly aware of the lock springing open in her door, then shuddered at the first contact of his lips on her hair.

What was he doing? His lips, warm in the cold winter air, touched the tender skin of her outer ear. All thoughts of what she wanted evaporated as she half-turned, resting her hands on his sheepskin collar and lifting her lips to touch his.

They were soft yet commanding, and she watched with fascination as his eyelids drifted closed, the long, dark lashes resting on his cheeks. His gloved hand reached up under her hair, cupping her neck, the gesture so familiar she felt like weeping as she leaned into him and her eyes slammed shut.

He tasted of coffee and a hint of toothpaste, but more than that, he tasted familiar. For years she'd forgotten that particular flavor, but now, it was like walking straight into the past. A taste that was only Jason Elliot, and it shook her to her toes.

Then he pulled back, released her hair and heaved a huge breath.

"I'm sorry," he murmured, and his long arm reached behind her to open her door.

"Me too," she answered quietly, sliding on to the seat as he shut the door behind her.

Sorry that it had ended so soon. And sorry that she'd come home. Everything just got a hundred times more complicated.

CHAPTER THREE

They were both silent on the drive back. Molly had nothing to say; her lips were still tingling from the taste of Jason's mouth on hers. She told herself they were quiet because Sara was sleeping in the back, but she was only fooling herself. She had no idea what to say to Jason at this moment. Her mind was effectively wiped clean. His hands gripped the wheel and he stared out the windshield, never glancing in her direction. His jaw, his beautiful rugged jaw, was set, hard and condemning. She wasn't sure if he was mad at her or at himself, and she didn't really want to find out. It was crystal clear he was angry, and she wasn't up to getting into it.

The kiss had been more, and less, than she'd remembered.

He drove down the hill on Regent Street, then turned down King, heading along the river, dark and black in the January evening. Molly looked around her, first at the cathedral then at the stately old Georgian homes on Waterloo Row and the stretch of shoreline, commonly called "The Green", which was not green at all now, but held an unearthly glow as the streetlights shone on the blanket of snow. When she'd been doing her undergraduate degree, she'd spent a lot of time in this part of town, going for beers at their favorite pub on Thursday nights, grabbing lunch from one of the small restaurants snuggled in between office buildings, or studying on a bench under stately elm trees. Now, driving past it in the winter dark, she felt so far removed from this town and that part of her life that she knew she had come back a stranger.

What must have been going through Jason's mind to make him touch her in such a way? And what equal madness had made her turn into his arms, lifting her face to his like a sunflower to the sun? It solved nothing, didn't change the past or the ways they'd hurt each other. All these years she'd thought they'd made a clean break, but twenty-four hours after her arrival home, and he'd already had his mouth on hers. It had to be simple curiosity—it was the only explanation that made sense.

When Jason pulled into Kim's driveway, Molly said softly, "If you'll take the keys and open the door, I'll get Sara." She was happy now that the little girl was between them, running interference. Having him walk her alone to the door would be too tempting, too frightening.

He held the door open wordlessly. Molly lifted the sleeping girl out of her seat and carried her gently into the house, sliding past Jason without meeting his gaze. Blearily, Sara woke as Molly tried to slide off her boots and winter jacket with as little fuss as possible. "Shh," she whispered. "We're home. Let's get you up to bed."

She looked at Jason as she hefted Sara into her arms again. "I'm putting her to bed. Thanks for the lift. You don't have to stay." Her voice coolly dismissed him.

He shut the door behind him, and she heard his truck start as she got to the top of the stairs. Then it finally dawned on her that he hadn't spoken one single word since leaving the hospital.

Jason slipped off his white coat and hung it on the hook on the back of his office door. All day at the clinic he'd seen clients and their pets, ordered lab tests, smiled and joked with his staff. He'd eaten a quick ham sandwich in the kitchenette in the basement, then had taken an hour to run the deposit to the bank and make a drop-off at the lab. An ordinary day.

Every minute of that ten-hour day, he replayed last night's kiss.

What had he been thinking, anyway? Molly wasn't the same Molly he'd fallen in love with as a teenager. He'd known that the minute he'd opened the door to her.

She was a hotshot lawyer now, making scads of money with a high profile oil and gas company. She'd waltzed back home in expensive clothes and an exclusive attitude. She didn't realize she'd become snobby, he was sure of it. But the years away had changed her. She acted like being back east was something to be tolerated. Like it was a little behind in terms of progress and sophistication. When she'd left for bigger and better things, she'd made it clear that Fredericton, that *Jason*, wasn't good enough for her. She hadn't wanted the life that he'd planned for them.

Yet for a moment, when he'd reached around her to unlock her door last night, he had been transported back to nearly a decade before. The smell of her hair, the feel of her body as she'd leaned back against him, just a little. Something they'd done a hundred times before. He'd nuzzled her hair and, carried away with the moment, had pressed a small kiss to her scalp, her ear. He hadn't expected her to turn and kiss him. He hadn't expected to kiss her back.

He hadn't expected it to feel like she'd never left.

The staff had all gone home, and it was only Jason and the kenneled animals left in the quiet building. He gave them one last check, then turned off the reception lights and set the alarm. He took out his key and, in the frosty air, turned it to latch the deadbolt. His breath formed clouds and he remembered the feel of her cold lips against his. That feeling, her taste... They were as familiar as if they'd been happening every day for the past six years. Kissing Molly had raised his pulse to a nervous hammering, had opened his heart until something similar to hope had slammed in.

He hadn't thought there was any room for hope in there anymore.

He knew there wasn't hope in there for Molly.

He shook his head and started up his truck, letting it warm up before putting it into gear. Kissing Molly had been a terrible mistake. Because hope was the last thing she could give him. And it was the last thing he wanted. She would only hurt him again. He knew that as surely as he knew he'd never truly gotten over her.

He entered the dark house, feeling a little lonely. He sighed, cursing Molly's return. For a few short days, it'd been nice to have Sara there with him, her bubbly chatter filling up the empty space and giving him a purpose.

All those years ago, he'd dreamed of coming home to Molly at night, to a warm, cozy house and their children. It had broken his heart to suddenly realize she didn't want those things, not the way he did. As time had gone on, he'd nearly forgotten how much he longed for a family of his own until the last few years, living next to Kim and Sara. Sara was a dream child— bright, precocious, darling. As he turned on the light, Bubbles trotted over. The little ball of white fluff was insanely happy to see him. He crouched and ruffled the dog's curly fur.

"Hey, you." He chuckled as the dog pushed her head against his hand. "You hungry?" He stood, filled the dog's dish from the bag in the cupboard and got her fresh water. It was nice having her here. The cats... They didn't seem to care much one way or the other when he got home. They only came running when he opened their food. But Bubbles greeted him every night. It was a poor substitute for a family, but he'd take whatever he could.

Heading to the fridge, he noticed the light flashing on his phone and stopped to push the button for his messages.

"Hi, Uncle Jason. It's Sara. Can I come see Bubbles tonight? Okay. Bye."

He smiled at the brief, uncomplicated message. Lonely didn't begin to describe how he'd felt recently. Sara was like a little ray of sunshine on a cloudy day.

But Molly would have to bring her over.

He took his hand off the phone. He had to get over Molly once and for all. Seeing her was torture, but he wasn't going to let that keep him from seeing his favorite girl.

Setting his lips, he picked up the phone and dialed.

He'd just finished eating a piece of sloppy, microwaved lasagna when the doorbell rang. Pushing his plate to the side, he rose to answer it, and his heart skipped a beat as he opened the door to see Molly with Sara in her arms. Molly's hair was pulled back in a simple, girlish ponytail, the ends trailing on the collar of her coat. Her cheeks were pink from the cold above the striped scarf wrapped around her neck. Sara's face was close to hers, close enough for Jason to see the resemblance—the blonde hair, same shaped eyes and the bow of their lips. By appearances, Sara could have been theirs, his and Molly's. Jason pasted a smile on his face to hide the quick stab of regret. "Hey, sweet thing. Let's go see if Bubbles is in the backyard."

He took Sara from Molly's arms and said quietly, "Come on in, make yourself at home."

He left her there, taking off her coat, while he carried Sara to the back door. Sara waited while he opened it and whistled, and a white, cold, snowy ball of fluff barreled into the house.

"Bubbles!" Sara sat happily on the floor while her puppy joyously licked her face.

"Why don't you take her out on the porch and play with her toys?" Jason suggested as Molly entered the kitchen.

"Can I, Aunt Molly?"

He looked at Molly, surprised that Sara had thought to ask permission. By the startled expression on her face, he could tell Molly was as taken aback as he was.

"Sure."

The two disappeared and within seconds giggles and squeaks from plastic toys erupted from the sun porch. Jason went to the table, removed his plate and took it to the sink. "So."

Molly laughed a little, tightly. "So. How was your day?"

Jason's eyes slammed shut as he kept his back to her and leaned against the sink. Such a normal question. But a question he'd once expected to hear every day of his life from this woman. The more she was around, the more he was reminded that she'd walked away from a life together. A life he'd wanted but she hadn't. Their life.

"It was fine."

Molly walked over to the door to the porch as uncomfortable silence fell between them, heavy and anxious. He stared at her stiff back.

Jason sighed. "Actually it was terrible. I'm sorry, Molly, I never should have kissed you last night."

Molly sighed, and the sound was filled with relief as she turned back to him. "I think I kissed you, but I agree it was a mistake."

They were in agreement. The words shouldn't have hurt, but they did. He met her gaze evenly. "It won't happen again."

"That's good. I came home to look after Sara and to help my sister. I don't need complications."

"I'm a complication now? How flattering." He didn't try to hide the bitterness in his tone.

Molly shoved her hands in her jeans pockets. Even in casual clothes, her manner of speaking, her posture, exuded control and purpose. She wasn't the carefree teenager he'd fallen in love with. She was every inch a corporate lawyer. He was surprised that it held a little attraction for him.

"I didn't mean it that way," she amended. "I only meant that I'm here for a short time and for a specific reason. In two and a half weeks, I'm flying back to Calgary and the life I left behind there. We both know that's the truth. We have to act accordingly."

"Does that life in Calgary include a relationship?" He turned to put his plate in the dishwasher, making his tone deliberately casual.

Molly's brow furrowed. "I can't see how that's any of your business."

"You're right. It's not. But I'm curious anyway." He shut the fridge door. "Is there anyone special?"

Molly thought about Christian. She supposed they could be construed a couple in the loosest sense. They attended company functions together, filled an appropriate need in a world that moved conveniently by twos. But there was no passion, no commitment between them. And they both knew it. It was how they wanted it.

"I'm not in love, if that's what you're asking."

"Why?" He leaned back against the counter, and Molly was struck by the fact that Jason hadn't changed, not that much. He was still calmly, coolly logical. Still sure of himself. And still sure he was right. He was simply an older version of the young man he used to be.

The young man she'd been in love with. She sat down at the table. Her first lover, and now he was prying into her personal relationships, somehow making her feel like something was lacking. Like *she* was lacking. It would be awkward under the best circumstances; under these, it was torture.

"I beg your pardon?" The words were icy and her lip curled as she looked up at him. He'd lost the right to pry long ago.

"Don't get all in a knot. I'm just curious. What's preventing you from being in love?"

She laughed sharply. "Lack of decent men out there?" At his pointed glance, she relented. She simply wasn't up to having another argument. "Oh, I don't know as anything is preventing me. I suppose I'm too busy. Things are usually so crazy at work, I either stay late or take stuff home with me. I don't have much of a social life."

"And that makes you happy?"

Their gazes locked for long seconds as the question echoed through the room. Was she happy? With her eyes drowning in his dark chocolate ones, she remembered lazy Sunday afternoons when they'd never even bothered dressing. They'd eaten omelets and toast and had studied in bed until the feel of his hand tracing circles on her calves had grown so distracting they'd take a "study break." Their lives had changed so much, but was she any less happy?

As they gazed deeply into each other's eyes, Molly knew she had to break the spell. They'd both agreed that kissing had been a mistake. The way they were looking at each other now made her want to leap at him and start undoing the buttons on his shirt, getting to the warm skin underneath. Which would solve nothing. She cast her eyes downward.

"Sure, I'm happy. It's what I always dreamed of."

Without asking if she wanted any, he filled the coffee pot and measured grounds into a filter. "I work ten- or twelve-hour days and come home to an empty house. I know what that's like. It's damned lonely."

"That's you. This is what I wanted, what I chose."

He didn't answer, and her fingers fiddled with the corner of a woven cream-colored placemat. It may have been what she'd chosen, but she couldn't admit to him that, truthfully, she'd never met anyone who had measured up to the standard he had set. He'd been her ideal—dark and handsome, kind, ambitious, an attentive lover. Yet his strength, his utter conviction, had been a few of the reasons she'd had to leave.

The coffee gurgled and spat as it brewed into the carafe. Sara could be heard giggling with Bubbles in the porch.

Jason filled a mug with the coffee and placed it, black, in front of her, then with a small smile put a sugar bowl and carton of coffee cream beside her right hand. "You always did put your career ahead of relationships."

She added sugar and cream, stirred, put down the spoon and stared up at him. "That's unfair. You wanted to chase your dream and expected me to fit in your plans where *you* wanted. What I wanted didn't matter. You refused to hear me, to see that my way could have worked, too."

"I heard you loud and clear. You made a choice and it wasn't me." He took another cup out of the cupboard for himself, his body language relaxed but tension flickered in his tone.

She pushed away the coffee and her voice rose. "You're still as bullheaded as ever. You still don't get it. It didn't have to be a choice. We both could have had what we wanted."

"A wife going off to a school half a country away isn't my idea of a marriage." He slammed his mug down on the counter, his voice agitated.

"And demanding to have everything your own way isn't any kind of marriage or partnership. I believe that's called a dictatorship!"

Sara showed up at the door to the kitchen, her little mouth pursed. "Stop fighting."

Jason was immediately contrite and went over to kneel in front of her. "Sorry, muffin. Your Aunt Molly and I were just talking. Hang on a sec."

He reached into a cupboard and took out a small red foil bag. "Here. I'm going to give you these for Bubbles." He took out three dog treats that looked like bacon and ripped them in half so there were six pieces. "We're not fighting, okay?"

Molly hid behind her coffee cup, taking several short sips and watching Jason deal with Sara. He was so much better with her than she was, and that made her angry, too. She somehow always felt like she was in the wrong. Like she always measured up short. It infuriated her that he was the only person who could make her feel that way.

Sara nodded, then disappeared back around the corner.

"What I do with my life now is none of your business," Molly hissed, keeping her voice low.

"You're absolutely right. I lost that right the day you walked out on us."

Molly placed her forehead on her right hand in exasperation. That day, he'd never understood that he shared the blame, and obviously he still thought he was completely innocent. "You still think it was all my fault. You think you're completely blameless. Sir Jason the Perfect."

"I asked you to marry me. You were the one who said no."

"Even you know it's not that simple. You presented me with an itinerary of our lives for the next ten years, then wondered why I didn't go for it."

His eyes threw daggers at her. "I offered you everything. You tossed it in my face! Now you come back to save the day. Good old Molly. If there's a job to be done, she's gonna do it, right? And boy, is she ever going to make herself look good. And when it's over, you're gonna leave. Because that's the other thing you do really well."

Molly pushed back her chair and stood, her hands on her hips and her lips thin. "You couldn't be more wrong. You're jealous. You're jealous because I came home to look after Sara and Kim, and that's your job, right? Dudley Do-Right is outdone by the woman who did him wrong. Not everything in life is a competition."

"If that isn't pot calling kettle."

"I call it as I see it, if you remember," she retorted.

"Be careful," he ground out between clenched teeth as they squared off.

She sniffed. "You tried to run my life once before. I didn't let you then, and I won't let you now. Get over yourself."

"Right back at ya."

She stared for a long moment, breathing heavily from anger and frustration, their argument firing her blood almost as much as his kiss had. She was appalled with herself for thinking how she'd love to close the distance between them and kiss him senseless. Rip off his clothes. She wondered if the sex would still be as spectacular...

Whoa. Too far. Time for a strategic retreat.

Spinning, she stormed to the porch. "Sara, say goodbye to Bubbles, honey. It's time to go."

"Aw, do we have to?"

Absolutely. "'Fraid so, kiddo. Gotta get you ready for bed. It's seven-thirty already."

Without saying a word to Jason, Molly stuffed Sara's arms and legs into her coat and boots with terrifying efficiency.

She opened the door, taking Sara's hand. Sara half-turned and called back, "Bye, Uncle Jason!"

Molly heard him call something, but she was too busy towing Sara across the yard to listen to what it was.

Molly flipped through the third file of the day and sighed at the cream-colored stack that still remained. This was the first time she'd had a chance to open her briefcase. Looking after one three-year-old was proving to be more challenging than negotiating land leases and royalty contracts worth millions of dollars.

She closed the file and slid her laptop over on the kitchen table. Clicking on her e-mail button, she waited what seemed like forever for her messages to download. Kim had a computer, but her internet access was spotty. Molly poured herself another cup of coffee while she waited. She opened a message from a colleague, but the words didn't register. All she could see were Jason's furious eyes as they'd argued.

So many feelings left to simmer. Molly supposed it was inevitable they'd vent them now after leaving them unresolved. But she hadn't been prepared for the reality of dealing with him again and confronting all those feelings. It was proving to be more intense than she could have imagined.

She had to stop thinking about him and focus. Sara would be asleep for perhaps an hour. Molly wondered how much work she could accomplish in that amount of time.

She was immersed in page seven of a contract when she felt a tiny hand tug at her sleeve.

"You're awake already?" She turned, pulling off her reading glasses, and rubbed the bridge of her nose.

Sara nodded and stuck a thumb in her mouth, something Molly hadn't seen her do before.

"Can you play for a little while? I need to finish this."

Sara looked up at her, saying nothing, but her brown eyes glimmered with tears and the thumb went deeper.

Molly sighed and pushed the contract out of reach on the table. "What's wrong?"

Two tears splashed over Sara's eyelashes. "When's Mommy coming home?"

Molly sighed again, then picked up the girl and placed her on her lap. "I'm not sure, honey. Probably in another week or so. She needs to be better so she can take care of you, right?"

Sara nodded, but Molly could tell she wasn't appeased.

She had work she must finish, but faced with Sara's tears, knew she'd have to finish it after Sara was in bed for the night.

She hadn't seen Jason in three days, not since she'd taken Sara to see Bubbles. She told herself that was not the reason for her short temper and irritability lately. After their fight, distance was certainly best.

"Tell you what. Let's make cookies."

Sara's head perked up immediately. "What kind?"

"What's your favorite?"

"Monster ones."

"I don't know what those are."

Sara hopped down, took Molly's hand and dragged her to the cupboard. "They have M&Ms and chocolate chips and stuff," she explained and opened the drawer next to the oven that held Kim's recipe box. "In there."

She lifted out the box. "We'll see." An idea blossomed. "But maybe we can make some and then sneak them in to your mom. Would you like to visit her again?"

Sara's eyes brightened further and Molly wiped the tears from the girl's cheeks, thinking how sweet and fragile her niece was. There was no contest. Work could wait. For now, there were cookies to bake.

With Sara's help, Molly found all the ingredients they'd need. She measured and Sara poured, and they took turns stirring. A little over an hour later, they had three dozen cookies cooling on a wire rack, and both aprons and four feet of counter were covered with flour and sticky oatmeal.

"What a mess."

Sara looked up, happy as a clam. "That was fun. I'm hungry."

"Let's test one." Molly poured them each a glass of milk while Sara picked up two cookies. They sat at the table munching away, Molly listening to Sara's animated chatter with half an ear.

Sara threw her arms wide, tipping over her milk. Molly jumped up and grabbed a towel, but not before a river of milk spread to the contract she'd pushed aside earlier.

"Oh no!" Frantically she mopped, but the bottom edge of the contract was soaked.

"Sorry, Aunt Molly," Sara apologized in a quiet voice.

"Sara, you've got to be more careful!" Molly held up the papers, trying to press the moisture out of them with her tea towel. She huffed out a sigh of frustration, then saw the girl dip her head and heard the sniff.

She shouldn't have yelled. It had been an accident. And Sara was pretty fragile right now.

"Sara, it's all right. Never mind, okay? It was an accident."

"But you're mad!" The words came out in a dramatic wail.

Molly smiled reassuringly in response to the drama. "Well, yes, a little. This is my work." She pressed a kiss to the girl's head. "But you didn't mean to spill your milk and I should have picked up my things. I'm sorry I yelled at you."

Sara looked up, hope in her innocent eyes. "When I spill stuff on Mommy's papers, she hangs them up with a clothes pin."

"Good to know." Molly ruffled Sara's hair. "Let's get this place cleaned up and go visit your mom while these cookies are still fresh."

❦

They drove to the hospital in the late afternoon, while daylight was disappearing, washed out against the white earth. Sara clutched a paper bag of cookies in her hand while Molly carried her purse and a paperback novel. They found Kim sitting up in bed, watching Oprah with headphones on, her hair clean and pulled back in a braid, her color much improved.

"Mommy!"

Kim's mouth opened in surprise as her daughter scrambled up on her bed, boots and all.

"Hang on there, tiger," Molly said and hurried to take off Sara's snowy boots. "Remember your mom's still sore, Sara."

"If you're gentle, you can snuggle right in here." Kim adjusted her weight gingerly, making room for her daughter close to her side.

"We brought you a surprise." Her chubby hand held out the bag.

"You're my surprise," Kim answered, but dutifully peeked inside.

"Monster cookies! My favorite."

"Aunt Molly and me made 'em."

"Aunt Molly baked? Glad I'm already in a hospital in case they have to pump my stomach." Kim sent Molly a teasing smirk. "They smell delicious. May I have one?"

Sara nodded. Kim dipped her hand into the bag while Molly sat in a vinyl chair next to the bed.

"How are things going?"

Molly smiled. "Okay. It's been a learning experience."

Kim laughed tightly so as not to jar her ribs. "When I called you, I remember you saying, 'How much trouble can one toddler be?'"

Molly let an affectionate grin crawl up her cheek. "Aw, she's not trouble. She's just busy. I don't know how you do it, and work, and keep your house looking like you do."

"You get used to it."

Molly didn't miss the wistful note in her sister's voice. "You miss being home, don't you?"

Kim leaned over and kissed Sara's warm curls. "Of course I do. I miss my own bed and I miss real food and all that. Not to mention my little muffin here."

"Any news on when we can spring you out of here?"

Kim shook her head. "Doctor says close to another week. My incision isn't healing as he'd like, and I'm still on pretty strong meds for the ribs and the headaches."

Kim looked down at Sara, who had snuck another cookie from the bag. "Here, sweetie," she said, placing her headphoneson Sara's ears and then changing the channel to cartoons. Sara looked up in wonderment, then glued her eyes to the screen.

"So how's Jason?"

"I wouldn't know." Molly's mouth pursed up like she'd sucked on a pickle. She was trying to avoid thinking about their last fight. She'd done pretty well with that, too. At least ten minutes at a time now.

"Trouble in paradise?" Kim smiled cutely, snickering at Molly's sour look.

"You're enjoying this far too much."

"Hey, I have nothing else to entertain me. I'm bored to death. What's going on?"

"He's mad because he didn't get to save the day."

Kim chuckled. "You two have always been insanely stubborn. Never able to see the other side of things."

"What do you mean?" How much did Kim really know about why they'd broken things off? Had Jason confided in her? Considering how close they seemed to be, it was highly likely. Molly studied her sister curiously. Would Kim lay the blame on her the same as Jason did?

"Why do you think I asked you to come? I could have made other arrangements for Sara. It's been six years since you left to do your law degree, and you still won't talk about him. Someone had to get the two of you together long enough to resolve things."

Molly bristled. "That's not your place."

Kim continued, undaunted. "He's lived next door to me for two years, ever since he opened the clinic. I know for a fact he's never gotten over what happened between you. He refuses to talk about you, and even when I bring up something, like how you got your new job or moved to a new apartment, he changes the subject."

"So?"

Kim sighed. "You broke it off and left. You never talked to each other about it. You just left things hanging. I know he wanted to marry you. I see him with Sara. He wants a home with a wife and a family of his own. He can't have that until he moves on from you."

"So you set us up?" Molly leaned forward in her chair, her elbows on her knees, trying not to think about the warm feelings that accompanied the fact that Jason still held a torch. "How could you do that?"

Kim shook her head. "You think I planned to get myself nearly killed and spend weeks in the hospital just to get you two to talk? For God's sake, Molly. The other driver *died*."

Molly blushed. Knowing now what had happened and seeing how affected by it Jason had been, she knew her accusation didn't hold water. "Of course not. I'm sorry I said that."

"Don't be too sorry." Kim chuckled softly. "Once I came out of the anesthesia, I wasn't about to waste an opportunity. You needed to come home. I needed help. Jason needs closure. I know neither one of you had that after you left."

"He told you that?"

Kim offered a lopsided smile. "It's not rocket science, kiddo." Her face clouded for a moment as if she were remembering something, then cleared. "Jason did confide in me once about your breakup. It hit him hard. It hit you hard too, even though you wouldn't admit it. I want to see things made right, that's all."

"At least you're not matchmaking." Molly relaxed, then narrowed her eyes as Kim looked away.

"Kiiiim?" She drew out her sister's name in warning.

"Well, would it be so bad?" her sister defended. "You both still care for each other. I'd like to have my only family closer."

"Oh, for Pete's sake," Molly breathed, frustrated. "I have my own life, he has his. That ship has *so* sailed."

"Isn't there some middle ground?"

Molly sniffed, remembering asking him for that very thing. "There's never been any middle ground with Jason. He asked me to marry him right after we graduated. He was going to Charlottetown for his vet degree and I had been accepted to U of T. He expected me to change my plans and follow him to Charlottetown to be the good little wife. He had our future all mapped out. I'd work while he finished vet school, and then he'd come back here and set up his practice while I did my law degree. I'd finish and practice for a year, he said, before I got pregnant." She ran her hand through her hair. "He had us in a house with two point five kids and student loans up the wazoo before we'd even headed up the aisle. I suggested we wait. I wanted to go to Toronto and do my degree. We were still so young, only twenty-one. I said we had lots of time. I wanted to get my career established before we had kids, and I thought perhaps somewhere else might be better for both our careers."

"And what did he say?"

Molly met her sister's bold look evenly. "He said that four years apart was no way to start a marriage and his wife would stand by him, not head across the country."

"And what did you say?"

"I said that there were things we both wanted, and maybe we could find a way to work it so we were both happy."

Molly sighed, remembering. They'd been sitting on his bed, the June morning sun glowing through the blinds. He'd gone to his dresser drawer and had taken out a black velvet ring box. But hearing what he had planned for them had made Molly feel like she was being tucked into that box, closed in and doing exactly what Jason dictated. They had argued. He'd tucked the ring into his pocket and their voices had risen until they were nearly shouting. And things had fallen completely apart.

"He said me with him was the only way he'd be happy, and it had to be that way. I left."

"That's it?" Kim stared at her sister. "You never spoke again?"

"No. I went to Toronto and did my degree, as planned. He did exactly what he planned too, only he did it alone."

Kim frowned as she absently stroked her daughter's hair. "You guys need to clear the air," she suggested. "Professionally you have what you wanted. But personally... I mean, you haven't been one for serious relationships and neither has Jason. He dates occasionally, but before anything gets serious, it's always over. You're holding each other back."

"Well, thanks, Dear Abby. I'd rather cut off my own tongue than talk about this with Jason again." Molly's tone was acidic and final.

Kim grinned. "I'm sure he feels the same. Jason's one of the best men I've ever met, but both of you are as stubborn as mules. Somehow, you've both got to let go of your pride and get past it. You both deserve to be able to move on with your lives. The way things are, you're both stuck."

Molly leaned back in her chair and crossed her legs. "Is that your official diagnosis, Doctor?"

Kim smirked. "I love both of you. I want everyone to be happy."

Molly examined her sister closely. Jason lived next door, did all sorts of odd jobs for Kim; she trusted him with her daughter. Molly wondered about Kim's real reason for wanting Jason to move on. What if all of this was to exorcise any remnants of feeling so he could move on with a ready-made homemaker and family? Kim certainly fit the bill much better than Molly did. She had a house, a darling daughter, made home-cooked meals and was an all-around nurturer. Molly couldn't help but remember how he'd said he'd been listed as her next of kin number. And she couldn't escape the haunted look in his eyes when he'd described the accident. What exactly were their feelings?

"Are you in love with him, Kim?" She asked it point blank, then held her breath for the answer.

Kim blushed. "Me?"

"You're awfully set on him moving on. Do you want it to be with you?"

Kim looked down, and Molly's heart jumped with dread that she was right. She should have been happy, but the thought of Jason kissing her sister was too hard to imagine. She didn't like the thought of Jason kissing anyone, actually. And that was just silly.

"No." Kim looked back up, her features soft. "I love Jason. He's made life much better by being my friend. He's a father figure to my daughter and a confidante for me. But I'm not *in* love with him, Molly. I've always known his heart was somewhere else. Just as mine is."

Molly sighed. "You're still not over the lowlife, are you?"

Kim aimed a warning look that said, *not in front of Sara.* Molly clamped her mouth shut. Why her sister was still hung up on Sara's father was beyond her. He'd up and transferred across the country without a qualm, had never contacted his daughter. In Molly's opinion, he didn't deserve the pedestal Kim put him on.

"Please," Kim pleaded. "Talk to Jason."

Molly nodded, saying nothing.

The nurse came in to check Kim's vitals, saving Molly from admitting that she and Jason had already kissed. And fought.

When Molly returned home, Jason's truck was parked in Kim's driveway. They hadn't eaten dinner yet and as soon as Sara saw the truck, she started squirming in her seat.

Molly shut off the car and rested her forehead on the steering wheel. Like it or not, for the next few weeks she was going to have to put up with Jason being around. And she was going to have to ignore the fact that he was still as sexy, maybe even more so, than he'd been all those years ago.

He opened the front door and stared out at her, making her heart pound foolishly. Her resolve was about to be put to the test.

CHAPTER FOUR

Molly took a deep breath as she pocketed the keys. Sara was practically bouncing out of her skin, seeing Jason filling the doorway. He was standing there like he owned the place, tall and uncompromising, and it made Molly immediately defensive. She should have known he'd have his own key, but it made her feel like she had when she'd realized that he was Kim's next-of-kin number. Now it seemed nowhere was safe from him.

She approached him coolly. "Something I can do for you?"

He looked down at her, clearly confused. "Kim called me. Said you needed help with the fuse box or something."

All Molly's aloofness evaporated as a laugh snorted out of her nose and she shook her head. Kim wouldn't let up, would she? "And you believed her?"

"It does sound kind of lame now, doesn't it?"

His deep chuckle warmed her and she glanced up to find his face more relaxed. She resisted the urge to reach up and touch the rough jawline.

Sara ran on ahead and took off her boots and jacket, leaving them strewn on the floor. Molly bent to pick them up before taking off her own coat. "I wish Kim wouldn't interfere."

Jason stepped all the way inside and shut the door. It seemed so...proprietary. Briefly Molly felt as if she was the visitor, even though this was Kim's house and she was the one staying here. Not to mention she now felt trapped in the tiny foyer with him.

"Interfere with what?" he asked, and she swallowed.

Her hands now empty of outerwear, she turned and let her gaze meet his. "She thinks we should talk."

"She would," Jason murmured with a tiny smile. "She'd expect us to sit down over a cup of tea and work it all out. That's her way."

From the sound of it, he heartily approved. Irritated, Molly couldn't stop the thought that Jason and Kim actually deserved each other... Mr. and Mrs. Paragons of Virtue.

But that wasn't fair—at least not to Kim.

"We tried that, remember? Only it was coffee and we ended up shouting at each other." And had upset Sara as well. Now at least her niece was around to run interference. Molly led the way to the living room, where Sara had already turned on the television and was watching a kids' program. The last thing she'd wanted after dredging up the past with Kim was rehashing it with Jason. She wished he'd just leave since he knew the emergency was bogus. She absently ruffled Sara's hair before speaking again.

"You know, it amazes me. She's nearly four, but she already knows every button on the remote control." She smiled, but it faded as she continued. "Anyway, I didn't tell Kim about the other night. I think it's better if we forget about it." As if they could.

He stood behind her, close enough that she could feel his warmth through her sweater; she felt, rather than saw, his shape and knew she would never really forget all the moments they'd shared since her return.

"Forget about the argument? I agree. It doesn't change anything."

"Perhaps we should forget everything that's been said and done since you opened your door and found me there." She focused on Sara as her heart paused, waiting for what he'd say next.

"Are you saying we should let the past go and start over?" His voice was soft in her ear and she shivered.

How many times had he murmured endearments in her ear over the years? For more than four years they'd been a couple; now she could hardly go anywhere without some sort of reminder of that time. Still, nothing affected her more than his voice, his touch. The thought of starting over was exhilarating and deathly frightening at the same time.

"Do you think that's even possible?"

He stepped back and the air around her felt suddenly cold, deprived of his presence. "No, I don't."

She turned, her heart heavy. What had been good between them had been *really* good, but all the things that had gone wrong were still there.

He looked down at her, his jaw set and his eyes cold.

"People always talk about a clean slate," he said, shoving his hands into his back pockets. "But you can erase marks on a slate. They haven't found a way to erase memories yet. And we have too many of those."

They stared at each other a long time as the past warred with the present.

"Do the memories still haunt you, Jason?"

He turned away, avoiding her probing eyes. Perhaps she'd gone too far. She had said all along that she didn't want to get into this with him. But now, now they were together, she couldn't help it. She felt the odd urge to know exactly how badly he'd been hurt. If he'd suffered as much pain as she had.

She laid a hand gently on his shoulder, which stiffened beneath her touch.

He stared at her fingers on his shirt. "What do you want me to say, Molly? You broke my heart when you left. For four years you had been my world and then you were gone. You never said goodbye. You never called or wrote. It was easy for you."

Easy for her? Never. Molly glanced at Sara and lowered her voice to a whisper. "Is that what you think? That it didn't hurt me to leave you?"

"You didn't show it."

"How do you know? This is the first you've seen me since I left."

He turned back to her and she saw the pain in his eyes, along with resentment and perhaps even a little longing. "Did it?" He took his right hand out of his pocket and cupped her jaw. "Did it break your heart to leave me?"

She swallowed, closed her eyes to the touch of his fingers on her skin. Oh, it had. It had torn her to little pieces and she was coming to realize she'd never really put them back together. Nothing had changed. Jason was still her ideal, no matter how much she blamed him for their breakup. But he could never, never know that. She couldn't give him any ammunition, not if she wanted to make it home in one piece.

"I survived," she whispered and exhaled as his hand disappeared from her face.

He cleared his throat gruffly. "I'd better get going, if there's no emergency," he murmured, and she let him go.

Molly sighed, took her fingers and began to work a kink out of her neck. Files were strewn all over the kitchen table, a cup of cold coffee sat forgotten beside the humming laptop. Sara had gone to her room to play tea party with her stuffed animals and Molly had grabbed the moment to get something—anything— accomplished. She'd planned to put in a few hours every day while Sara napped. But that hadn't worked out, as at this age naps were the exception and not the rule. The briefcase sat unopened and she'd spent her time picking up toys, soothing hurts and doing laundry. Now she was trying to play catch-up on a Saturday.

She cocked an ear. Sara was being awfully quiet. Too quiet. Frowning, she wondered what sort of trouble the toddler could be into. She glanced at her watch, realizing with surprise that it had been over an hour since she'd opened her briefcase. Where had the time gone?

She headed for the stairs as a strange feeling of unease began to pulse through her. Perhaps Sara had grown tired and fallen asleep.

When she opened Sara's door, she knew immediately the girl was not there. It was silent, too quiet. Animals were scattered on the frilly pink spread and a handful arranged around the play table with cups and saucers before them, but there was no sign of any other occupation in the room. The unease grew to a frantic pounding of her heart as she opened the closet and checked under the bed, in case Sara was hiding. But she found nothing beyond a few missing Barbie clothes and an unmated sock.

"Sara?" she called out, but her voice echoed throughout the house. She felt, rather than knew, that something was not right. Still, she rationalized as she hurried out of the room. Sara was only three. She couldn't be far. She was probably just hiding, looking for some attention. It was Molly's fault for trying to focus on work.

She checked the other bedrooms—nothing. She ran down the stairs, checked the living room, the laundry room, even the pantry. No Sara.

"Sara, if you're hiding, come out. This isn't funny." Her voice cracked on the last word and she felt anger war with the fear running through her body. *I should have watched Sara more closely*, she berated herself. That was the whole reason she was here. She skidded to a halt in the entry. How could she explain to her sister that she'd lost her daughter? In her own home?

That was ridiculous, she rationalized. Sara had to be here somewhere. Molly took a deep calming breath, trying to think logically.

Her eye caught Sara's pink peg where she normally hung her jacket. The peg was empty and the boots that usually sat so precisely beneath it were gone, too. One pink mitten lay orphaned on the floor. Her stomach hit her feet. In what seemed like slow motion, she looked at the front door. The deadbolt was unlocked.

Disregarding her own coat, she threw open the door and called, "Sara? Sara, answer me!"

Nothing. The snowman they'd made earlier that week was leaning lonely to one side, one rock eyeball laying on the ground. The only sound was the soft shush of thick snowflakes fluttering to the ground.

Oh God. How could this have happened? The thought skidded through her brain as she pulled on her jacket and shoved her feet into Kim's winter boots, leaving them unlaced. Sara wasn't in the house. Her coat and boots were gone and she was somewhere in a snow flurry with only one mitten. What if she'd decided to try to see her mother?

Visions of Sara walking along the busy road by herself nearly stopped Molly's breath. Anything could happen. She could be hit by a car; no one would see her in this visibility. Or someone could stop and take her. She could get lost and be out in subzero temperatures before they found her. Tears of terror pricked Molly's eyes and burned the top of her nose. Sara was gone and it was all her fault.

Don't panic, she commanded herself and told herself to breathe. After she inhaled, then exhaled, she knew there was only one person she could call for help: Jason. Jason would know what to do.

She ran through the ankle deep snow to his house and pounded on the door. "Jason? Jason, open up! It's Molly!"

He threw open the door, looking harassed with his mouth set in a firm line and his eyebrows pulled together in the middle, making a crease in his forehead. "Keep your shirt on!" he ordered, frowning down at her.

At the sight of him, she started to cry without explanation. It didn't matter that she had vowed not to need his help. It didn't matter that they were still at odds over broken hearts and mixed messages. All that mattered was that Sara was missing. All she knew was that there was one person she could count on. Could always count on.

"Please," she begged, her voice thick with tears. "Sara's gone and I can't find her anywhere and her coat is missing and..."

Jason grabbed her upper arms. "Get a grip, Mol," he ordered. "She's here. She's asleep on the couch."

The flood of relief almost buckled her knees and was immediately followed by hot anger. Anger at Sara for disappearing without telling her. Anger at Jason for not calling to let her know. And most of all, anger at herself for losing it in front of him. Tears pricked again, relief and confusion and frustration all rolled together in one uncontrollable, blubbering mass.

"What in the blue blazes is she doing over here? And why didn't you call to tell me?" She wiped her cheeks furiously, leaving them tearless and blotchy.

His chin flattened. "Now it's my fault?"

"I thought she was in her room!"

He stood upright, indignant. "And I thought you had let her come over. That's what she said."

At that Molly's eyebrows soared sky-high. "I wouldn't let her come over alone! What sort of person do you think I am?"

He sighed, and his shoulders slumped a little. "The kind that would take great pains to avoid spending any time with me."

Silence dropped like a bomb. Standing back, he pushed open the door so she could enter.

She did and took off her coat, not knowing what to say. He was right, after all. She had been avoiding him. She peeked inside the living room to the right. Sara was laying peacefully on the sofa, covered with a soft blanket with a gigantic golden retriever's face on it.

Watching the girl sleeping, Molly took several deep breaths to get under control. Tears smarted in her eyes at the supreme relief of knowing her niece was okay.

Finally, she faced Jason. With her voice clogged with unshed tears, she said quietly, "You still should have called me. You have no idea what went through my mind. I was terrified."

"I'm sorry," he said quietly. "She said you'd said it was okay. I figured you'd dressed her up and made sure she got here. It's only across the lawn."

"I did not do any such thing. I was working in the kitchen and she was supposed to be upstairs in her room. I can't for the life of me figure out how she got out without me hearing."

"Well, she's safe, anyway," he said, and Molly felt the emotions draining from her slowly.

As the panic subsided, Molly caught herself staring up at him. She noticed for the first time what he was wearing, and her mouth watered despite the fear and anger still trickling through her veins. Bare feet and a pair of surgical scrub bottoms, paired with a white T-shirt. A day's growth was on his face. He looked relaxed and cuddly and she wanted to grab the drawstring on the front of his green scrubs and untie it. Pull him closer to her and feel his warm, hard body against hers. Let what was left of the adrenaline drain away in the shelter of his arms.

"That's the main thing," she whispered in response. Her aroused gaze lifted from the string to his face and she saw color creep into his cheeks. She'd embarrassed him, and the knowledge made one side of her mouth twitch.

Still, only four feet separated them, and the urge to touch was strong. Molly felt her jeans hugging her tightly, felt the tightness of her bra straps as she became aware of everything in their tiny sphere of existence. She saw Jason flex and unflex his right hand, and she wanted to feel it cushioning her neck as he kissed her silly. She saw his chest rise and fall beneath his T-shirt and wanted to feel that chest against hers. The memory of it was so strong she could almost feel it now, warm and hard and smooth.

It took no longer than a heartbeat. Each took a step and a half and they were in each other's arms. As she'd imagined, Jason's right hand captured the back of her head as it had thousands of times before, while the other wrapped around her back and pulled her close against his hard chest. His mouth was firm and hot against hers and she pressed closer, losing herself in his taste and texture, and confirming that nothing had changed. They were still a perfect fit.

She lifted her hands and threaded them through his dark hair, leaving trails in their wake as he stepped her backward, pressing her against the foyer wall. His hips pinned her there while his tongue danced with hers. He made a soft sound in his throat and she felt a current run from her breasts to her core. Only one thing passed through her mind as his hand slid up her ribs. Sara was asleep.

At that moment, she felt something vibrate against her pelvis.

"Of all the rotten timing," Jason muttered, tearing his mouth away from hers. He reached down, took the cellphone from his pocket and looked at the number.

Molly stared up at him, her eyes dazed as desire coursed through her body. Oh no. In another few minutes, he could have carried her to bed and she wouldn't have put up a fight. Not one ounce of opposition. The thought exhilarated and frightened her all at once. Would making love to him now be the same as it had been? Better? Would all their anger and recriminations fuel it to burn even hotter?

Yeah, until they were both completely obliterated by the flames.

She could not lose control with Jason. She could not. Things were already too messy. She was absolutely going back to Calgary when Kim was better. What had she done?

He scowled at the phone and she saw his lips were puffy from kissing, his hair untidy. She lifted her fingers and touched her own lips. They were still humming from the force of his mouth on hers. The rest of her was resonating like a plucked string.

"It's the answering service. I've got to call in."

She nodded jerkily. "I should wake Sara. She and I have to have a chat anyway."

He sent her a look that said he was sorry they'd stopped. It said this wasn't a good idea. It said things were growing complicated. It said I don't want it to end here. She felt his lingering touch in that moment, even though his hands were no where near her skin. It was tempting to say the hell with it all and simply launch herself back in his arms.

"Go," she whispered, and with one last complicated look, he disappeared. A second later, she heard his deep voice on the phone.

She went to the living room and stared at Sara's sleeping form for a few moments. It seemed no matter what steps she took to avoid Jason, someone, something was always there, pushing them together. It wasn't fair. She'd spent years building her own life apart from him. He'd done the same. But now, in a few short weeks, she was right back there again. Wanting him more with every breath. Caring about him. Their lives entangled.

It had to stop. She'd built the life she wanted. She leaned over and shook the little girl's arm lightly.

Jason hung up the phone and headed to the living room. Stopping in the doorway, he grinned at the stern tone in Molly's voice as she sat on the edge of the sofa. She'd be so good with kids of her own, he thought, and his heart stopped for a moment before beginning to tick again. Molly didn't want kids. Or more precisely, she didn't want *his* kids.

He stepped inside the room and heard Molly say, "You can't do that. You are absolutely not allowed to leave without me with you, and especially not to go alone. I was worried sick!"

"I'm sorry, Aunt Molly." The girl lifted honest brown eyes to Molly's. "I wanted to see Uncle Jason and you'd say no." Her little voice was clogged with tears.

"Why would you say that?" Molly's voice was puzzled as she questioned Sara.

"You always fight. When Mommy's home, we visit all the time!"

Kids had a way of seeing things clearly, Jason realized. He approached and knelt beside the couch, speaking sternly. "Look, kiddo, you knew you were doing wrong, because you lied to me about it. You told me your Aunt Molly said it was okay."

"I'm sorry, Uncle Jason. I'll ask first next time."

"You'd better." He tapped his cheek. "Give me some sugar."

She placed a kiss on his cheek. He saw Molly try to hide a smile at his quick capitulation. He didn't care. He knew Sara a whole lot better than she did. Sara was a good kid who'd been through a lot and had made a bad decision. She was also the kind of kid who rarely needed tough discipline, a good talking-to was usually all that was required.

"I've got to go into the clinic," Jason told them. "I could use a hand. There's a hit-by-car coming in. The staff has already left for the day, and I'd hate to call one of them back."

He wanted her to help at the clinic? "What about Sara?" Surely she should stay back and look after her niece. Molly thought about nursing a bloody animal and her stomach lurched.

"We can put her on the sofa in the compassion room. She'll be fine. She's right at home there. Aren't you, muffin?"

Molly knew she wasn't going to get out of it, and she'd look like a queasy coward if she refused. The way his eyes were imploring her right now made it difficult to say no to anything.

"All right. Let's go, Sara."

A beige sedan was already parked out front when they arrived. As Jason unlocked the clinic door and disengaged the alarm system, Molly held the door for the distraught young couple carrying the limp animal.

Molly asked Sara to show her the clinic while Jason got started. Sara led her through an open area with counters and stools and a refrigerator, past a tiny washroom and down the stairs to a small room decorated in calming cream and blue, complete with a low sofa, a chair, a large coffee table and a small TV and DVD player. It was the perfect place for a little downtime for both staff and clients.

"Can I watch a movie, Aunt Molly?"

"Sure, pumpkin." Molly opened a small cabinet and perused a selection of kids' movies. She picked an old Disney favorite. "You okay here by yourself for a while?"

Sara nodded. "I play here when Uncle Jason's working. He has juice boxes."

Molly kissed Sara's head and smiled. Sometimes she could be so self-sufficient. It continually amazed Molly. "I'll check on you later, okay?" But Sara already had her eyes glued to the screen.

Jason was in an exam room when Molly came back to the work area. He was bent over a limp and muddy brown dog, whose claws scratched on the stainless steel table with every disoriented movement.

"Grab a coat off the wall and a set of gloves," he commanded, and silently Molly slipped into a white coat, buttoned it up and pulled her hands into stretchy latex gloves.

"Hold right here," he said, and she gripped the dog's leg as she was told, staring at the spot that he'd already shaved clean of hair.

Molly watched with fascination as the vein popped up beneath the V shape of her hand and Jason inserted the needle, hooking in an IV.

He rubbed the dog's head affectionately, and Molly got a glimpse into Jason's dedication and compassion. He'd been right to make this his profession. He wasn't just competent, he was caring. Far more understanding than he could show to people sometimes.

"There you go, Casper. That's a good boy." He ruffled the dog's ears lightly.

"What's next?"

He carried Casper to the X-ray room. Molly slipped the heavy iron apron he gave her over her clothes and helped position Casper on the table. The dog cried out as she moved his left hip. When Jason looked at the films, he showed her where the break was in the dog's leg. He left momentarily to talk to the owners, explaining Casper's injuries and his course of treatment. Molly stayed in the exam room, patting Casper's head. She had a look around, impressed. Jason had been out of school for only a few years, but it was obvious he'd worked very hard at setting up his own clinic. It was clean, orderly, complete with state of the art equipment, yet with a comfortable, homey touch for his patients' owners.

He came back with the young couple behind him, their faces lined with worry. "He's a bit out of it," Jason explained, but smiled reassuringly. "But that's

because we've made him a little more comfortable. He's going to be just fine. I promise."

They patted Casper and whispered endearing words to him as he lay quietly, groggy with pain medication, his tongue hanging limply out of his mouth.

"We'll set the bone and stitch up his lacerations," Jason explained warmly. "Why don't you call back on Monday to check on his progress? We'll settle your bill when he's ready to go home."

They nodded, and the woman bent to kiss Casper's brown head. "Thank you, Dr. Elliot." She smiled at Molly who smiled back. "And thank you for coming in on a Saturday."

"It was no problem," he answered, but his gaze cut to Molly and she remembered very distinctly what the after-hours call had interrupted.

"Molly will show you out," he suggested, asking her with his eyes if she'd mind. Without a word, Molly led the couple to the door. After they were gone, she locked the deadbolt behind them and made a quick check on Sara. The movie was still running, and Sara had helped herself to a cheese and cracker snack. Her head was on a needle-pointed cushion and she'd covered herself with the throw from the back of the couch.

When she returned to the exam room, Jason was finishing setting the bone. Casper's mouth was open and his tongue lolled out. "Boy, he's out of it," Molly remarked. "Does he feel anything?"

Jason smiled a little at her concern. "Not much."

"What will you do with him tonight?"

Jason pulled over a tray. "He'll be fine here, and tomorrow morning Jan comes in to walk and feed the animals. She'll make sure he's fine, eating and peeing and such."

"Oh."

"He's lucky he's not hurt worse," Jason continued. "This is nearly done. How's Sara?"

Molly took the clear plastic bottle he offered and irrigated the wound as he indicated. She found gauze on the tray and dabbed it a bit while Jason prepared to suture the laceration.

"She's fine. She got a snack and covered herself up."

"She's a good kid."

"Mmm. Except when she takes off without asking."

Jason chuckled. "Yeah. Except then." Carefully he began stitching, and Molly marveled at his perfect sutures. His hands moved smoothly, almost poetic in their grace. Molly glanced up and saw the concentration on his features.

Oh dear.

She was getting hooked on him all over again, and that was too dangerous.

The whole afternoon they'd worked together in harmony. Molly had felt none of the resentment she had expected, nor the nausea. Instead, she'd followed his lead and had learned a lot without the strained atmosphere that seemed to surround them elsewhere. When Jason was here, doing his job, he was uncomplicated. Efficient and kind and competent, without ego. She looked down at his neat stitches, rinsed the wound again. Her coat had splatters of blood on it; she didn't care. She'd actually enjoyed this afternoon. There had been no arguments, only conversation. But enjoying Jason was simply not in her life plan. It became too easy to forget all the reasons why she'd left him in the first place.

"This is nice," he said quietly, mirroring her thoughts. Her stomach jumping, she stared at his hands making stitches rather than look in his eyes.

"Yes, it is. I don't enjoy fighting with you."

"Sure you do." His fingers kept stitching evenly, but Molly knew if she looked up, he'd be wearing a half smile that popped his dimples.

"Well, maybe I do." She dabbed at the wound and smiled a little.

"You always did," he continued, his fingers squeaking slightly in the latex gloves. "We used to have some spectacular arguments. Remember the time we went camping at Mount Carlton? You were determined to go for a swim in the lake after hiking. I told you that you'd be a mess of sticks and it wouldn't clean you up."

"I remember," she murmured, recalling all too well. They'd gone for the swim. She'd gone on and on about how refreshed she'd felt. Back in their tent, she'd peeled off her suit to discover her entire body covered in little sticks and bits of grass. They'd collapsed laughing. He'd picked the sticks off her skin and made love to her in the day's waning light.

"I also remember us fighting over Elizabeth Lawrence." His voice held a note of teasing.

"Yeah, and it was me who was right that time. She was dead gone on you. You were so blind I thought I was going to have to hold her down and shave her head to get her to leave you alone."

"You would have, too."

"Damn right."

They laughed together, then it faded.

In those days, she would have fought for their love.

"Our arguments never lasted long, though."

His voice was strangely thick as he answered, "No."

Her hands paused—her first mistake—as the words *make-up sex* raced through her head. Quickly, she grabbed the water bottle and applied it again. They had always made up, except for that one last time. And like that time camping, it usually had involved both of them getting naked.

As Jason threaded his needle again, she knew instinctively he was remembering as vividly as she.

He cleared his throat. "We're almost done here. Why don't you round up Sara?"

"Are you sure?"

"I'm just going to make this guy comfortable," he said, rubbing the dog's ears. "I'll check on the rest of the crew in the back and we can go."

Molly was part way out the door when his voice stopped her. "Mol?"

She turned, finally meeting his gaze.

It was a mistake. The instant that their eyes met she knew he'd been remembering, too.

"Thanks for your help today," he said quietly.

"You're welcome," she answered and spun from the room before she could say something she'd regret.

CHAPTER FIVE

She hung her lab coat back on a hook and threw her gloves in the garbage before going to get Sara. She found the little girl sipping happily on a juice box as the end credits of the movie scrolled through.

"You've been good. You ready to go?"

"Yup. I had a powernap. I'm hungry."

Molly laughed. "Let's talk to Jason. Maybe we can convince him to let us have a treat."

Together they tidied up the room so it was as neat as it had been when they'd arrived. When they went upstairs, Jason was coming out of the kennel room. "You ladies ready?"

"Uncle Jason, can we go to McDonald's?"

His gaze darted to Molly, and she grinned widely. He sighed, clearly outnumbered. "Drive-thru only, kiddo. I'm too much of a mess to go anywhere. We'll take it home, okay?"

Sara jumped up and down, tugging on Molly's hand. "He said yes! Yippee!"

Molly angled an amused look at Jason. "Someone has lots of energy. She had a *powernap*."

"Let's go, then. She's always quiet when she's eating."

They drove to the McDonald's in Oromocto, and then went back to Jason's house to eat. Molly set Sara up at the table and went to find Jason. She discovered him in the laundry room amid piles of sorted clothes awaiting his attention. Being a single guy with his own business obviously did not leave a lot of time for domestic chores. She could relate to that. Her laundry basket was constantly full, and there always seemed to be a layer of dust on her furniture thanks to fourteen-hour days. If she got her promotion, she was seriously considering getting a maid to come in once a week.

"Aren't you eating?"

He blushed. "I've gotta change first. This shirt's covered in blood and mud." His dirty bottoms were sitting in a heap on the floor; he now wore clean jeans, but the scrub top had streaks of blood and mud in the pattern of doggie toenails. "I forgot to get a shirt."

"Do you want me to get it?"

"Do you mind?"

She'd been looking for an excuse to snoop through his house. So far she'd only seen part of the downstairs. "Nope."

"T-shirts are third drawer down in the dresser."

"I'll be right back." She left him spraying a prewash treatment on his pants.

Upstairs she found his room. It was dark in the late winter afternoon and she flipped a switch, which turned on a bedside lamp. The bed was made haphazardly; the covers thrown over top of the pillows without much precision. Molly ran her hand over the end of the spread before going to the dresser.

Had he said second or third drawer? Molly hesitated, then curiosity got the better of her and she pulled open the top one. It was, as she expected, his underwear drawer. Cotton briefs, a jumble of sports socks and three neatly folded pairs of dress socks looked up her. Rapidly she pushed the drawer back in.

She opened the next drawer. It was filled with scrubs, some green, some dark blue. She pressed her hand down on the pile of shirts, hitting something hard and square with her hand. She dug beneath the clothes, pulling out a black velvet box. It was familiar—too familiar—and her heart began beating a strange tattoo.

With shaking hands she lifted the lid. The hinge creaked softly in the twilight. Nestled inside was the engagement ring he'd bought for her all those years ago.

It winked up at her, a shining, painful reminder of that day years before when he'd offered it to her and she'd turned it away. That was the one fight they'd had that hadn't been resolved. Yet he'd kept the ring all this time.

With a trembling finger she reached out, touching the bright diamond in the center, flanked by two smaller ones. Why had he kept it? It was an uncharacteristically sentimental thing for him to do. He'd been so angry. She'd always figured he'd gotten rid of it right away. But here it was, sitting in his dresser. A lover's memento. Or a hurtful reminder of mistakes.

He was waiting for his shirt, she realized, probably wondering what was taking her so long. Not wanting him to catch her with the ring, she hurriedly closed the box and shoved it back under the shirts where she'd found it. She grabbed a T-shirt from the next drawer and exited the room, leaving on the light.

At the bottom of the stairs, she halted.

She could see Jason still in the laundry room. Transfixed, she watched as he peeled the scrub shirt over his head and tossed it in the washing machine.

His upper body was absolutely stunning. Each muscle curled into the next, all shadows and curves and dips. He'd always been lean, but in the intervening years he had indeed filled out to be...most impressive.

Her hand gripped the banister as a grand rush of desire flooded through her. This was not supposed to be happening. They were still as different as they ever were, perhaps even more so. Hers was a life of power suits, of legal briefs and corporate dinners, while his consisted of scrubs and labs and fast food on the run. His house was comfortable with curtains that didn't quite match and cookie jars that stood empty.

Her condo was done by a decorator with coordinated accoutrements.

Her life was across the country and his was here. But knowing it didn't stop the wanting. Didn't stop the wondering of why he'd kept her engagement ring, or what that could possibly mean.

Taking a breath, she descended the last three steps, gripping his shirt in her fingers.

He looked up at her approach. Mesmerized, she took one step, then another, closer to him until they stood face to face. She could feel his breath on her skin; see the rise and fall of his chest as his breathing quickened, matching her own. In that moment she regretted, for the first time, the decision she'd made six years ago. This body, this man, this heart—the one she would swear she could hear beating—could have been hers all along.

"I brought your T-shirt," she whispered, then stared at his lips. They were perfectly bowed and slightly open, and the fleeting memory of them on her skin haunted her.

He took the clean shirt out of her hands, then dropped it to the floor. Without missing a beat, he framed her face with his hands and pulled her roughly to him, staring at her lips so intently it was almost as though he were already kissing them.

"We shouldn't..." she breathed.

It was like dousing a fire with kerosene. His fingers slid down her neck and dug into her arms as he plundered her mouth with his. No niceties, no gentle tugs and starts, just raw, pent-up passion.

He danced her across the floor until they reached the laundry room door. Blindly, his mouth still fused to hers, he shut it and turned the handle, locking it.

She had no choice. Her hands slid over the skin on his chest, devouring it, memorizing it. It *was* different. Bigger and harder and, dear God, much more manly. The man he had been was but a shadow of the one he'd become...and she'd loved the first with all her heart. As his hands cupped her breasts, she knew it would be even harder to walk away from the man he was right now.

His fingers left her breasts and reached for the button of her jeans. She sucked in her belly, allowing him access, moaning as he licked her neck and plunged his hands down inside the backside of the denim. He pulled her closer, moved to untie his own drawstring and she panicked.

Molly pulled away frantically. The kiss at the hospital had been a surprise and the one earlier had been a misguided response to a tense situation, but this one wasn't right. Despite the demands of her body, the need that pulsed through her at this moment, it would be a mistake. It would change nothing for her... She was still Molly the Lawyer who was here only for three weeks. But for Jason—he still kept the ring he'd given her so long ago. She wouldn't, couldn't, trifle with his feelings. She knew as surely as she knew she wanted him that to give in would cause regret on both sides.

"No, Jason." She put a few feet between them, her chest rising and falling heavily with repressed desire. In the intervening years, her temperature had never risen to this level, not with any man. Jason had only begun to touch her and she was feeling like she was ready to combust.

"Are you saying you don't want this?"

She tried to laugh but it came out shaky and far sexier than she wanted. She clamped her mouth shut, trying to think of the right response. "I'll admit my body says yes," she said finally. "But my heart and my head won't let it go there."

He came closer and she backed away, finding herself pinned between his body and the wall. "Jason," she warned.

He leaned forward, teasing his lips over her earlobe. "Just one more kiss, Molly," he whispered, making all the fine hairs on her body stand at attention.

An image of the ring floated before her eyes and despite any regrets she might have to the contrary, the decision had been made long ago to end their relationship. No good could come from rekindling it now. She knew that deep down. She'd made her life. This was a *complication* she didn't need. It didn't matter what she wanted.

One more kiss would be one too many.

"Nothing's changed," he murmured, his breath warm on her hair. His body slid closer until she could feel his hips pressing against hers. "I still want you, Mol."

His words did the trick. She could get lost in heated actions but admissions of lust had the power to make her stop. She pushed him, squirming away from his arms and the eyes that seemed to see how divided she was.

"But it's different now between us. This wouldn't solve anything."

His eyes burned bright across the few feet that separated them. "I know. It doesn't stop the wanting. It doesn't stop me from wanting to make love to you."

Her heart spun about in her chest. "We moved on." She struggled, unsuccessfully, to keep her voice steady.

"You moved on. I'm still here."

Everything swirled around her as the impact of his words struck her. Had he been stuck in the past all this time? Together with the knowledge of the ring it was too much. If she wasn't careful, next he'd be saying she'd made a mistake and should never have gone to Toronto. And if she wasn't careful, she'd be agreeing with him. She twisted her hands around each other nervously.

"I can't do this. I can't."

"I know you can't."

Her hands stilled. What this was all adding up to was hard to believe. "Are you saying you've never gotten over me?" Even to her ears, that sounded incredibly conceited, but after what he'd said, what she'd found, she had the burning desire to know.

"What if I haven't? We both know that in another week or so you're heading back to Calgary. And, yeah, maybe this isn't wise, but right now I'm not exactly thinking with my head, you know what I mean?" He stood before her, all lean muscle and snug jeans and her stomach flipped.

Lust. It was just lust and perhaps a little nostalgia about how good it had been between them. He wasn't asking for forever. He was asking for a fling. It was a horrible idea that couldn't have a good ending, and it was unlike him to even suggest such a thing. That knowledge made it a little easier for Molly to pull further away.

"We've left Sara far too long."

Jason stared at her for a long moment, his chest heaving. It seemed he couldn't shut off his body any more effectively than she could. Molly let out a breath she hadn't realized she'd been holding as he leaned over to retrieve his shirt from the floor. Her mouth watered. *Traitor,* she grumbled inwardly, staring at the worn patches on his jeans pockets.

There was a knock on the door, and they both jumped.

"Uncle Jason? Bubbles needs to pee, I think."

Molly avoided his eyes. "You put your stuff in the washer. I'll get Bubbles." *And then I'm getting out of here,* she thought. She couldn't deal with this right now.

She opened the door, trying to keep her face pleasantly normal for the three-year-old. "Let's let Bubbles outside, okay?"

Sara followed Molly to the patio doors. As the washer started filling, Molly slid open the door and grabbed Bubbles' chain.

"What were you and Uncle Jason doing in there, Aunt Molly?" Sara's voice was sweetly innocent.

"Laundry," Molly replied, and her hands fell still.

In the old days, Jason's apartment had had laundry facilities in the basement, which had meant leaving the apartment for each separate load. On lazy afternoons, while making love, they'd ignore the ringing of the phone, and when asked, they'd always say they'd been "doing laundry."

It had been a long, long time since she'd done laundry with Jason. But she could feel it as if it had been yesterday. She'd admit it to herself now, how close they'd come to doing it again not ten minutes ago.

"How come your face is all red?" Sara persisted, and Molly's smile faltered as she felt her face color further.

Jason emerged from the laundry room, fully clothed and forcing a smile. "Did you eat *all* the food, muffin?" He ruffled Sara's hair and glanced at the plate with the remnants of a chicken nugget and a few fries stuck in ketchup.

"Nope. Just mine. I got a puzzle in my kid meal."

"Cool. Guess I'll nuke mine."

He glanced in Molly's direction. "Mol? Heat yours for you?" His voice was coolly polite, as if the hot little scene in the laundry room had never happened.

She wanted to say no. But Sara was looking up at her with those pleading brown eyes and she didn't have the heart to simply take off. "I guess. Thanks."

Molly felt nothing like eating but knew she should anyway. The fries were soft from the microwave, the lettuce on her sandwich limp from reheating. But at least her pop was still icy cold. The food filled a hole and gave them something to do in the silence.

She dipped a soggy fry in ketchup and frowned. Why did it have to be him, and why now? He had kept her engagement ring all these years. Safe and snug in a dresser drawer, in the original box. What could it possibly mean? Did he take it out and wonder what if? Or look at it as a reminder of their spectacular failure, a talisman against further mistakes? She looked over at Sara taking the puzzle from the wrapper. Did Jason ever think they could have had a child like Sara?

At the time, she hadn't wanted to think about children, and he'd planned it out.

She started making a list in her mind of all the things that needed doing. Work had always been her shield, and it had been effective. She'd go home and get to work, and the whole Jason problem would disappear.

"Penny for your thoughts."

His voice intruded as Sara busily went to work on the puzzle, her eyebrows knitted together in concentration. Molly took a sip of her soda, avoiding the question as long as she could.

"You don't want to know what I'm thinking." And even if he did, there'd be icicles in you-know-where before she'd tell him. She was thinking he was still carrying a torch for her, a big one. She didn't know what to do with that. She didn't want to hurt him again, of that she was sure. But it looked like she was bound to no matter what she did. They'd already gone too far.

"Perhaps I do."

She stood up and carried her garbage to the receptacle beneath the sink, avoiding the eyes that seemed to follow her everywhere these days. "A girl's gotta have *some* secrets," she joked weakly, pasting on a smile.

He brought over his own garbage and used it as an excuse to lean in close against her back, his mouth only inches from her ear. "You can't deny what just happened in there," he whispered.

His breath fanned her earlobe and she shivered. "No, of course not. We were both there. But thinking that changes anything...would be a mistake."

She cringed at how cold her voice sounded, but it was necessary. She didn't want Jason. What she wanted was for Kim to get better so she could go back to Calgary and get on with things.

He pulled away. "You're right, of course. You've made it abundantly clear you are only here for a few weeks and then it's back to your previously scheduled life."

Using that cold tone back to her was effective. Despite feeling closer at times, right now she knew they'd never been further apart. It should have been a safe feeling. Instead it made her want to apologize. And not just for tonight. She'd been quick to blame Jason for their breakup, but she carried her own bit of guilt with her. She'd run away. He was right about that. She had packed up and left town without a word, no explanation. The years they'd spent together had deserved more. A better ending. She was ashamed now at how she'd handled it, yet she had no idea how to make amends without making it seem as if she was asking for something.

"Mol?"

She shook her head and turned to see Jason watching her curiously.

"Where did you go just now?"

"A long way away," she replied. She tucked her hands in her pockets. Now was no time to think about closure. Not with Sara here and not when she could still feel his fingers on her skin. "We'd better get going. I'm cleaning house tomorrow. Kim comes home soon and I don't want her to see a war zone."

"The clinic is closed tomorrow. I was hoping the three of us could do something together."

She had to look away from the hope in his eyes. "I'm not sure that's a good idea."

"Why?"

Her voice was low with warning. "You know why."

He looked over at Sara taking the puzzle apart to start again and then back at Molly. "Just an afternoon of something fun. Like sledding, perhaps. There's this hill over at the university..."

"I know the hill," she answered sharply, a little too sharply. Of course she remembered the hill. They'd gone tobogganing there as students, getting cold and wet and, afterward, heading to the SUB—the student union building—for a hot drink. The two of them and some of their friends, laughing and having a marvelous time. Another on a long list of memories.

"Forget it then."

"Jason, I'm sorry. I didn't mean to be short with you. This is all just weird for me," she tried, but knew it was a lame attempt at explanation.

"The past is the past, Molly. I thought Sara might enjoy a fun day out, that's all. Hey, for that matter, I can take her myself and then you can get some work done. Don't worry about it."

Then why, suddenly, did she feel like she was being manipulated?

CHAPTER SIX

Jason took advantage of his morning off to visit Kim alone. The hospital was hushed, with few visitors on her ward. When he slipped inside her room, she woke from a nap with a smile.

"Hey, neighbor," she said with a groggy tilt to her lips.

"Hey, yourself. Sorry I woke you. Should I go?" He gestured back toward the open door.

"Absolutely not."

He took off his coat, draped it over a chair and then pulled the chair next to the bed. "How're you feeling?"

"Stiff. Annoyed. I am not healing fast enough. I want out of here like yesterday." She scowled.

"You're doing fine." His gaze lit on the bouquets of flowers that were past their prime. "You want me to do something with those?"

Kim followed his gaze. "Keep the cards for me? I'll get housekeeping to do something with the vases."

He nodded, falling silent.

"Something on your mind?"

"Yeah. You can guess what."

Kim laughed a little, careful not to jar her ribs too much. "I figured as much. Surprised you haven't been in earlier. She giving you grief?"

"I know we needed her to help with Sara, but I wish she'd never come."

Kim reached over and took his hand, squeezing. "Dredging up the past isn't fun, is it?"

"It's torture," he confirmed.

"We both know you can't use me to hide anymore, though. Don't we, Jason?"

He looked down at her bruised, pretty, understanding face. Kim knew things. She knew what had happened six years ago, but she'd never assigned blame. She'd listened, making room for him in her life when he was lonely and full of wishes. She'd filled a spot in him and he'd tried his best to do the same for her. It hadn't been easy on her, bringing up a baby all by herself. No father. No parents around, no sister to pamper and indulge her. In a way, part of the anger he felt toward Molly had to do with how she'd abandoned her sister as well. Like their mother had when she'd remarried after their parents divorced. And Molly should have known better.

"I know that. I just…needed to see you today."

"What happened?"

"Before or after I seduced her in the laundry room?"

Kim coughed, choking on a sip of water. "You guys had sex?"

"No…well…almost. It was a close thing."

"You stopped." Her eyes narrowed. "Then what happened?"

"I propositioned her. Suggested a fling, can you believe that?" His cheeks heated even as he admitted it.

This time Kim couldn't hold back the laugh. She snorted and grabbed her sore rib in response. "An affair? Oh, my. I wish I'd been a fly on the wall. And…"

"And she turned me down flat. What was I thinking, Kim?"

Using the bed rails, she pushed herself up to a half-sitting position. "You weren't thinking. Or you were, but not with your head." Her teasing grin faded. "You guys never said goodbye, so the past six years have been prolonging that. Neither one of you has a clue

how to deal with the other, so you're feeling your way
around. And it's probably easier to fool around than
actually *talk* about it."

"How did you get so wise?" He crinkled his eyes at
the corners. "You always could do that, put things in
perspective," he added. "And I love you for that.

For the past two years, Kim and Sara had come to
be family. He wasn't such an idiot that he didn't know
why. Their relationship had begun with her as a
replacement, a stand in, pure and simple. She was
alone and raising a daughter, and at first he'd been
happy to help. She'd always been nice to him when he
and Molly had been dating, showing none of the baby
sister jealousy he'd expected. After the break-up, he'd
thrown himself into his studies, but once he'd come
back home to start his own practice, he'd started
thinking about family again. The family he wanted.
The one he'd thought he would have with Molly. To
find Kim next door with a baby had filled a need. At
least then he'd been able to pretend he wasn't alone.

"Nothing going on in my own life," she said, tongue
firmly in cheek. "Makes seeing other's lives pretty
clearly."

Jason didn't know how she did it. Work full time
and raise a daughter, and do such a great job at it.
He'd admired her so much at first that one night after
fixing her washer, he'd briefly—ever so briefly—
considered taking it further.

He'd kissed her goodnight.

On impulse he'd turned at the door and pressed his
lips to Kim's, hoping something would be there.

Instead, she'd pulled away, confused, shocked and
they'd both started laughing. It simply wasn't right.
She wasn't Molly, and he couldn't pretend that she
was. Sara's father still held a special place in Kim's
heart. They both had known it in that moment. And
knowing there would never be anything physical
between them, knowing they had their wounded

hearts in common, had cemented their friendship. It went deeper than any friendship he'd ever had, certainly far more honest. He became Uncle Jason, getting his "family" fix from her and Sara, and being there to help Kim with the challenges of being a single parent. Now Sara was as dear to him as any daughter could be.

"So what do I do now? Forget she's here?"

Kim sat up as her lunch tray was delivered, placed on the swiveling table to her right. "You get through it. You let her go, find a way to make peace with it. Because I don't think she's going to stay this time, either. She's going to stay until I get out of here, and then she's going to go back to that job of hers. I don't want you to get hurt all over again. Either of you."

He knew by the sinking feeling in his heart that Kim's warning was right. Molly wouldn't stay, not unless he could show her what she'd missed. But did he really want her to? Or was he simply trying to resolve what had been left unfinished? Was he trying to prove to her that he'd been right all those years ago?

"I can handle it," he assured her, even though he wasn't sure himself. "Listen, I've gotta go. I'm taking Sara sledding this afternoon." He stood abruptly and snagged his jacket from the chair, avoiding her gaze as he left out the fact that Molly was going along with them. He leaned down to place a quick kiss on her cheek. "You're a lifesaver, Kim."

Blandly she dipped her spoon in red Jell·O. "Yeah. And next time make it up to me with something edible, okay?"

He flashed her a smile as he hit for the door.

At one o'clock sharp, Jason lifted the tailgate and slid the toboggan into the back of his SUV. Perhaps he was being stupid, or crazy, but he had a day off, Sara had been without her mother for what must seem like forever to a child, and the snow was perfect for sledding. If Molly wanted to act like she had a stick up her butt that was fine. He wasn't about to let her stop him from spending time with Sara.

He thought about the backhanded confession he'd made to Kim this morning. In some ways it might have been easier if he could have put Molly behind him and had fallen in love with her sister. He'd hoped, but even then Molly had been the specter he couldn't exorcise. Instead, he'd found a best friend, the sister he'd never had.

When he knocked he heard music pumping loudly through the door. What the heck? Didn't Molly have any respect for the child's eardrums? He tapped his foot, ringing the bell again. When it too went unanswered, he knocked hard with his fist. The volume dropped and seconds later the door opened. Molly, still dressed in some sort of pajamas, had her hair gathered in a rat's nest on her head and held a dust cloth in her hand.

"Jason!"

Was this Molly, the corporate professional? Her pajama bottoms were flannel and blue, with white puffy numbered sheep on them. The top was a plain white T-shirt with what looked like a blob of peanut butter smeared above her right breast. She was less than even casual, and more approachable than he'd seen her since she'd arrived. And more alluring.

"I came to take Sara sledding," he got out, and she moved to the side to let him in.

"Aunt Molly, see me dance!"

The cry came from the living room and Molly's answering smile was swift. She went to the doorway while Jason quickly removed his boots and followed. He looked over Molly's shoulder, chuckling despite himself. Sara was dressed in a fluffy pink confection of a dress, play heels on her feet and a tiara atop her curls, spinning in circles with her teddy bear. Jason realized now that the music in the background wasn't Molly's. He thought he recognized the song from Cinderella, but wasn't sure. Molly's free hand was over her mouth, holding in her mirth at the princess-ballerina.

Jason stepped into the room, made an exaggerated bow and held out his hand. "May I have this dance?"

"Ooooh! Uncle Jason's the prince!" With a giggle, Sara held out her hand, the regal princess. He hefted her up and twirled her around the room. Maybe he looked silly, but he didn't care. Sara loved dancing, and she was getting too big for Kim to pick up anymore. At the end of the song, he put her down, bowed again and then advised her it was almost midnight.

When he turned back to the doorway, Molly was watching him with curiously soft eyes. His cheeks warmed beneath her gaze. For a second, it almost seemed...but no. Molly hadn't wanted children. She hadn't wanted a domestic life. She still didn't. This was just cleaning day and Sara was simply being too cute. The little girl could warm the coldest heart, he knew. Including Molly Shaeffer's.

"Again, Uncle Jason! This time I'll be Ariel and you can be Eric."

He lifted her again, unable to resist her sparkling brown eyes, and swirled her exaggeratedly in sweeping circles.

"Aunt Molly, too! Dance with us, Aunt Molly!"

Startled eyes met his across the living room. His words were cool, but he offered, "Sure, come on in."

She stepped into the awkward embrace, her left hand on Jason's shoulder beside Sara and her right loosely clasped in his palm. Sara snuggled in, contentedly sandwiched between them as the music frilled around the room, but Jason was swamped by an

overwhelming feeling of déjà vu. He'd danced with
Molly hundreds of times, and even with Sara between
them, it still felt the same. Intimate and sweet, their
feet moving to the music around the room. It was with
relief and a real sense of self-preservation that Jason
stepped away as the song ended, avoiding meeting
Molly's eyes.

"Hey, muffin, I came to take you sledding, but I'm
afraid the princess dress isn't going to cut it."

The teddy bear was dropped unceremoniously to the
floor. "I can change. Can't I, Aunt Molly?"

"Yes, you can. Your clothes are on top of your bed."

With a squeal, Sara skidded out of the room.

"The invitation still extends to you, you know," he
said into the silence left by Sara's exit. His hand still
tingled from the feel of her palm in it.

She avoided his eyes, going instead to tidy up CD
cases. "I probably should finish up here."

"Leave it until tomorrow. Good sledding doesn't
happen every day, you know," he cajoled. "We'll never
get a more perfect day. Besides, you know Sara's going
to ask you to come. You might as well stop fighting it
and get ready."

"Oh, all right." She put down her dust cloth. "I
suppose one afternoon out isn't going to kill me."

She was halfway to the door when he tossed out,
"Hey, this is supposed to be fun. Remember? It's not
like you're walking to the gallows. Leave your bad
attitude at home."

He heard her mutter something under her breath as
she headed for the stairs and he laughed. Teasing
Molly, knowing which buttons to push, had always
been so much fun. He'd known how to do it back then
and hadn't forgotten. When Kim had first suggested
Molly come, he'd dreaded seeing her again. He'd told
Kim at the hospital he'd wished she'd never come, but
he knew deep down that wasn't true. Now he was
starting to realize he was glad she'd come home.

They'd supposedly been over for a long time, but their chapter had remained unfinished. Now, by getting closer, perhaps they could put to rest the ghosts that had haunted them all this time. Leave each other with some good memories instead of a bitter aftertaste.

"Uncle Jason, I need help."

He jumped when Sara's voice intruded from the foyer. How long had he been standing there? Hurrying out of the living room, he saw Molly coming down the stairs wearing the ski pants to Kim's set. Sara was on the bottom step, doggedly trying to pull her pant leg down over her boot.

"Here, honey, I'll do that," he said, kneeling before her while Molly scooted around him and retrieved her own boots.

"We set?"

"Yeah!" cried Sara, and Jason laughed.

"Toboggan's in the truck. Let's go."

The big hill, the one Jason and Molly had loved, was crowded with teenagers and university students with toboggans, Krazy Karpets and saucers. Molly laughed as one inventive boy sat on the blade of a steel shovel, holding the handle in front of him for steering. Jason looked down at Sara sitting on the toboggan while he pulled it and decided the hill next to it was a bit gentler and better for Sara's size.

"Over there?" He lifted his chin toward the area, and Molly nodded in assent.

The afternoon was alive with chirping birds and the squeal and swish of sleds and inner tubes rushing down the hills. Jason reached the top and took a minute to straighten his back from tugging Sara up the slope. Some things seemed timeless, and seeing the hill crowded like it always had been years before

took him back. They'd done this often. They'd spend
the afternoon sledding, then head to the pub for some
hot chocolate and Bailey's to ward off the chill. But in
the years since he hadn't found any joy in the sport.
Now that Sara was old enough, he welcomed the
feeling of anticipation, the way his breath clouded on
the air, the screams of those brave ones behind him
hurtling down the steep hill.

"Pumpkin, you ready?"

Brown eyes peered up at him anxiously from above
her scarf. "I dunno."

"I'm going to sit right behind you, okay?" He looked
up at Molly, her face obscured by a puff of air as she
exhaled. "You give us a push to get started?"

"Sure."

He sat on the long wooden end of the sled, tucking
his boots near the front curve and keeping Sara
cradled safely within his legs. It had been years since
he'd gone sledding, and childish glee rushed through
him as Molly's hands pushed against his back and the
toboggan began to move.

"Hang on, kiddo!" He looped the yellow rope around
his gloved hands and away they went, skimming over
the snow, the wind cold on their cheeks as the bottom
of the hill rushed nearer and nearer. Sara squealed,
Jason laughed, then all too soon they slid to a stop.

By the time he reached the top again, he was out of
breath. "You're heavy for a little mite," he quipped,
then aimed a deadly smile at Molly. "You're next."

He'd expected resistance, but got none. With an
impish grin, she tucked herself around Sara. *What the
heck?* he thought, and sat on the end of the sled,
looping his legs over so his boots rested in Molly's lap.
She held the rope and he used his knuckles to push off,
laughing at Molly's "whoop" as they slid even faster
this time.

At the bottom, a fir tree came rushing towards them
and Molly tried valiantly to shift her weight and turn

the toboggan, but to no avail. When they were close enough to see the needles on the branches, Jason shifted his weight to the left and they tumbled over into the hard white snow.

Legs, arms and rope were all entangled as they caught their breath, then Sara started giggling hysterically. "That was fun. Do it again!"

Jason became very aware that Molly, while off the toboggan, was still nestled between his legs. Her hat was askew and her cheeks were bright pink from the cold and laughing. For a moment, it was as if the past six years hadn't happened at all, and they were simply Molly and Jason, the couple, out for an afternoon of fun. In this kind of situation, he would have pinned her to the snow and kissed the tip of her nose, promising all kinds of retribution for later. He stared into her eyes and knew she was remembering, too. Perhaps that had been the true purpose of this afternoon. It was a chance for her to see the past, to remember without rancor the kind of relationship they'd had. The kind of person she'd been—carefree and fun. Maybe what they really needed was to be able to remember the good times instead of the bad ending defining all that had been. Years of good memories had been clouded by a bad ending. It was easier to remember them when they were like this.

He dragged his gaze from hers and put on a cocky grin. "Since you made us dump, you get to haul her up the hill."

"Me?" Molly's lips thinned in indignation. "You're the one who tipped us, you creep."

"Maybe. But if you'd done a better job of steering, I wouldn't have had to save your necks at all."

She blustered as he blithely he picked up the sled, dumped the excess snow off of it and slapped it back down before walking away.

"You're going to pay for that," she warned.

He heard the hiss of them following behind and laughed. "Whatever, Mol. You don't scare me."

At the top of the hill, he needled her further. "Why don't you and Sara go alone this time? I think my extra weight made us go farther. That way you won't be near the trees."

"Yeah, just me and Aunt Molly!" came the cheer from the sled. Sara clapped her hands.

Molly smiled up at him, baring her teeth. "Chicken."

Gamely she sat, and he noticed she could actually tuck her boots right into the curve of the toboggan. He'd forgotten how small her feet were. He remembered them now, delicately arched and always with painted nails. Her eyes gleamed up at him from Kim's black and grey suit. "Coward," she whispered, taunting, while he grinned back at her like a fool.

He wasn't opposed to taking a little teasing either. In fact, in teasing each other, he felt closer to her than he had since she'd arrived. "Be careful who you're calling a coward," he warned with a wiggle of his eyebrows.

"We'll see."

"Need a push?"

"Go for it."

He put all his weight into pushing them, skidding in his boots and tripping, landing on his belly in the snow as Sara and Molly hurtled down the hill.

He watched, half laughing at himself, half at them when they hit a dip, got some air and tumbled over and over in the snow, finally landing in a brilliant pouf of white, unmoving.

His heart hit his throat as his face froze. Oh God. They weren't moving. "Mol?" he shouted, leaping to his feet. "Sara?"

As that single second of panic passed, he realized a tumble like that couldn't cause any real damage. Heading down the hill, he heard a giggle and a quick shhh and knew they were up to something. Stealthily he bent, scooped up a mitt of snow and molded it in his glove. *You're going to pay for that,* she'd warned, and he couldn't help the feral smile that curved his lips. If it was a fight she was spoiling for, she'd get it.

"Ambush!" went up the cry. Molly sprang to life, leaping from her position, hurling a snowball and hitting him square in the chest. "I'm not tugging her up there this time, Elliot! *Coward!*"

Sara's laughter bubbled over the thin, cold air as he laughed freely. "That all you got, Shaeffer?" He took aim and let his own fly. Then ran over the snow, boots squeaking, to catch her around the waist, preventing her next throw. Instead she twisted, crushing the snowball and squishing it squarely in his face, rubbing it in and giving him a washing.

Quicker than he thought possible, he grabbed her wrist, hooked a boot behind her foot and tripped her, pushing her into the snow and landing on top of her heaving chest. He sat up, straddling her, and stared down into her face which had gone utterly blank with surprise.

"Don't..." she warned him, her words a shaky stutter in the cold afternoon.

His voice was soft, deadly. "Don't what? Don't wash your face? Don't start what you can't finish, Molly m'girl." His lips were teasing, his eyes flashing fun as he raised a snow-filled hand menacingly.

Her eyes changed from shock to fear. Not of his strength, of that he was sure. But because she was realizing, as he did, that she still mattered. Discovering there was still so much between them, and he was torn between knowing this should be the end and the increasing realization that it felt like a beginning. It wasn't what he'd wanted and she'd made it clear it wasn't what she wanted either. But there it was, and he had no idea what to do with it.

He let the snow in his hand flutter back to the ground as his smile faded. He was used to being in control of situations and knowing this one was rapidly getting out of hand only added to his confusion. It was far easier to be angry at her.

"That was a stupid, childish trick, and you know it." His voice was silk lined with steel. "That sled popped up in the air and I saw Sara fall out first. She's so small... For a moment, my heart stopped."

"It was only a joke," she answered, her voice small and childish in response to his criticism, her jaw jutting out defensively. Sara grabbed the rope to the toboggan and tried to turn it over to clean it off.

He clapped a black glove to his forehead in exasperation. "What am I going to do with you, Molly?"

She didn't answer but stared up at him with wide eyes. He became acutely aware of the intimacy of their position as he sat squarely on her hips.

He braced a hand on each side of her head, dropped his gaze to her mouth and followed with his lips.

They were cold in contrast to the warmth of her mouth, and he poured everything into that punishing kiss—his anger, his hurt, his confusion over what was happening between them now. Her hand rested on his left thigh as he pressed more weight into her, feeling all the pressure points where their bodies connected. This couldn't go anywhere, it couldn't. He had to stop it, now. They'd only get hurt again, the voice of reason intruded. But his heart spoke louder, and for once, he listened. He took the kiss deeper, darker.

Molly had known by the look in Jason's eyes what was coming, but she hadn't been prepared by the force, the passion, the anger that poured from him into her. She didn't know what was happening to her lately, only that they kept hurting each other without even intending to. She rested her hand on his thigh, desperately trying to keep up with him as his body pinned her to the hard, snowy ground and his mouth translated his frustration.

Seconds ticked by and his lips gentled, prodding instead of punishing, deep, soul-searing contact that spoke to her more clearly than his words ever could. He didn't hate her. He cared. Cared more than she wanted to admit to herself. Not only cared...but had probably never stopped. All that was said, and more, as they kissed in the icy snow.

She gently pushed against his shoulder and their mouths parted a few inches, their breath creating frosty clouds, a white nimbus around their faces.

In another week, she'd be returning to her life as a corporate lawyer. They still didn't have a future, but they did have a past to finish.

Molly turned her head to the side and saw Sara standing watching them, her lips formed in a perfect 'O'. One hand held the rope to the toboggan, the other outstretched, pointing towards them.

"You kissed Aunt Molly," she whispered.

Molly's face heated. Goodness, she'd completely forgotten about Sara standing there, and what a show they'd put on, making out in the snow. Certainly not something appropriate for a three-year-old!

Her gaze shifted to Jason and he was blushing as furiously as she was sure she was. He pushed back, swung his leg over Molly so he was kneeling beside her.

"Well now, I guess I did." His self-deprecating laugh rippled over the freezing air. "You guys gave me quite a scare."

"Molly and Jason sitting in a tree," Sara began the chant, her eyes alight with impish glee. "K-I-S-S-I-N-G! First comes love, then comes..."

"Where did you ever learn that?" Molly demanded, scrambling to a seated position, stopping the song before Sara got any further.

"In day care," Sara explained nonchalantly. "Cody kissed Katie and Brianna taught it to me."

Jason cleared his throat while Molly fought to keep a straight face. "Honey, Jason and I have known each other a long time. He was worried we were hurt, that's all."

Sara hopped around, obviously enjoying the moment. "When you get a boo-boo, you get a Band-Aid," she explained.

"And a kiss better, right?" Jason lunged forward and scooped the pink bundle into his lap. "You hurt anywhere, muffin?"

"Maybe here." She lifted an elbow, which Jason dutifully kissed.

"And here." She touched her nose, and Molly choked out a laugh as the tot fairly simpered.

"You're a flirt," Jason confirmed, but kissed the tip of her nose anyway. "Let's get this sled up the hill. What do you say?"

"Okay. I'm ridin'."

They stayed another half hour for Sara's sake, but there was less laughter and more tension between them as they went up and down the hill. Molly couldn't escape the ramifications of the kiss, the feel of his stubble against her cheek or the way she'd been able to read his feelings. They'd always been like that, understanding each other without words, and Molly wasn't prepared to deal with what Jason had said to her today. They both kept saying they were over, but she knew that was a lie. She had to put some distance between them until she could figure out what to do. The fact that there was anything to figure fazed her more than anything else.

Finally, Jason called it quits. He sat wearily on the snow. "Last one, kiddo. My poor legs can't haul you up anymore."

They piled on the sled, one behind the other, and Jason pushed them off. At the bottom, Molly felt him rest his forehead against her knitted hat, his breath warming the back of neck as he sighed heavily, just for a moment. Then he untangled his legs from hers and lifted the toboggan to carry it to the truck.

She met his eyes as she took Sara's mittened hand.

"We need to talk," he murmured low enough so only she could hear.

Talk? She couldn't make sense of her own feelings, let alone his. The only thing she could do was pretend she hadn't heard him.

CHAPTER SEVEN

They went back to Jason's house for hot chocolate, at Sara's request.

After that kiss, all Molly wanted to do was disappear and brood, but Sara was demanding treats, and Molly knew the rest of the day would be a disaster of pouting niece if they didn't give in. Hopefully, there'd be no time to talk. Molly simply wasn't prepared. How could they possibly work things out when she didn't even understand her own feelings?

Jason made cocoa from scratch while Molly watched him from across the room. He frothed the milk with a wire whisk while Sara romped with Bubbles and Molly put out a plate of store-bought cookies. In some ways Jason was unpredictable, but in others...

Oh, in others. The way he kissed hadn't changed at all. He had a style, a taste that was simply Jason, one she was helpless to resist. One that was as natural to her as the sunrise each day. As he brought the steaming mugs to the table, topped with fluffy white marshmallows, she swallowed hard to stop remembering. To stop wanting him again.

"I only filled yours half, muffin," he explained, putting the cup before Sara. "But you can have more if you want it."

Sara happily munched on oatmeal raisin and sipped her cocoa, using a finger to dab at the white blobs on the top. Silence fell, heavy and awkward, until Sara finished her snack and headed for the living room and television, clearly subdued after her busy afternoon.

"Mol..."

She stopped him with a look as she cleared mugs off the table. "Not now. I can't talk about this now."

"Then when? Because we should talk about what happened. Today and the other day, too."

She aimed a furtive, frustrated glare in his direction. "Nothing happened, okay? Nothing that can happen again."

"We can't pretend it didn't happen, Mol."

"Yes, we can!" She turned her back to him, rinsed the mugs and put them in his dishwasher. She wondered how his voice could sound so calm and rational when everything was churning up inside of her. "We can because it changes nothing!"

"Aunt Molly!" The shout came from the living room followed by a tiny giggle. "You were pretty!"

She met Jason's bland stare and he shrugged, so she followed him into the living room.

Sara was in the middle of the sofa, her chubby hands holding a white-covered photo album in her lap. "Look." She pointed, obviously enthused. "Aunt Molly's pretty dress. And you have funny hair, Uncle Jason!"

Her angelic face looked up, having fun with an album Molly never even knew existed. One that Molly would rather not look at, but she didn't have the heart to take it away from Sara, not when the girl was having so much fun with it. She couldn't expect a child to understand what she herself could not.

They sat down, one on either side of Sara, with a book that was a visual diary of their years together. The picture she was pointing to was their prom. Jason in his black tuxedo and she in a long blue gown, a corsage of white roses adorning her left wrist. Pictures of the two of them and friends they'd long since lost touch with. Other pictures from their final year of high school, when he'd lived in rugby shirts and jeans, and she'd had her hair permed into a blonde, unruly mass. There was one of them at a school dance, her arms around his neck and his resting on her waist as they smiled for the camera. Another of them at the school Christmas drive for the local food bank. At a skating party with their group of friends. Sara asked what each one was and Jason dutifully explained while Molly swallowed back sadness as the memories trickled in, warm and painful.

Jason's mind drifted back as he touched a picture with his finger. This one, their hair damp and both of them dressed in oversized sweatshirts after a beach party and bonfire at the provincial park. That night had been the first night they'd made love after a year of dating. He'd known with all the wisdom of his eighteen years that he loved her, and that night, in his two-man tent, they'd gone *all the way*. It had been better than he'd expected. His nervousness had melted away the moment he'd held her warm, soft body in his arms and kissed her. He'd been her first. And she his. They'd learned all that they knew together.

For the next four years, they'd been inseparable, completing their first degrees and falling even deeper in love.

He flipped the page in the album and stopped.

He'd taken a photography course in his third year and as a joke, she'd modeled for him, hamming it up for the camera. He'd captured a few that he remembered now he'd kept, showing no one but putting them in his own personal album. One where she was laughing at something silly, her eyes and nose scrunched up and mouth wide with hilarity. Another of her sleeping after he'd loved her thoroughly, her hair rumpled, lashes laying long and full in slumber. Her cheeks were flushed and the silk strap of her ivory nightie was brushed off her shoulder, the sheets wrapped around her hips.

"Aunt Molly, you look just like Sleeping Beauty," Sara breathed.

Molly laughed, the sound coming out husky and shy. "Thank you, sweetheart."

"Was Uncle Jason the Prince that woke you up with a magic kiss?"

How could they resist such a guileless, enchanting creature? Jason watched as Molly put her arm around Sara and squeezed. "Yes, baby, he was."

Their gazes met and delved deeply. No matter how hard they tried to pretend, how much Molly protested, nothing was over between them. Not even close.

He looked away again and turned a final page.

This was the one he'd loved the most, the one he'd forgotten entirely about until seeing it again. He'd developed it himself in the dark room at school. Experimenting with black and white, he'd taken a picture of her beneath the arch at the Christmas Ball in their fourth year. Her hands held her long skirt in her fingers as she had half-turned. She'd worn white that night, a strapless bodice and full skirt, looking more like an angel than a woman had a right to. When she'd looked over her shoulder at him like that and smiled, he'd captured it. He'd wanted to re-create that shot, but on their wedding day, perhaps with her bouquet hanging loosely from one hand as she held her skirt, and a few strands of hair loose after their long day.

Sara's hands clapped. "You look like a bride!"

Molly swallowed hard. A bride that had never been.

She rose abruptly, avoiding Jason's probing gaze. "I just remembered I have some phone calls to make." The excuse was lame. It was Sunday. He had to know there were no calls, but he let her go.

"I'll bring Sara over later," he offered quietly. "We can talk then."

She didn't wait, didn't want to think about his persistence that they hash this all out. Right now she had to escape before she made an absolute fool of herself.

Molly looked around the house one last time, making sure everything was perfect. The appliances gleamed, the floors shone. Sara's toys were tucked away in a corner of the living room, stuffed into a yellow tub. A batch of cookies filled the cookie jar on the counter top and fresh sheets were on the beds.

Jason had volunteered to pick up Kim, leaving Molly time to ensure everything was done and dusted. Molly was growing quite used to the homey look Kim used with her decorating, and in the back of her mind even preferred it to her own precise, if somewhat sparse, decor. This house was a home. The furniture might have been mostly secondhand and unmatched, but Kim had a knack for taking nothing and making it look as if it *belonged.* Handmade accents added to a sense of intimacy. Molly's condo was a showpiece, no personality. It had all the proper decorations, color coordinated and in the right place... Classy by all standards. It was incredibly perfect and lonely.

It was like living in monochrome and moving into color. And, Molly would admit to herself, her life reflected it.

She ran a hand over the secondhand dining table, following a beam of sunlight on its surface. For years now, she'd told herself that her career was all that mattered. That she didn't want marriage and a family. She'd avoided home, telling herself she didn't have the time. Now she knew the real reason why. Home scared her. Being with Sara, seeing how wonderful a daughter she was, how great Kim was at being a mom, being with Jason again, letting old feelings carry her away. The way he cupped his hand around her neck when he kissed her, or melted her with a simple gaze across a snowy hill. It made her *want* things, things she had already given up and had no right to anymore. Things that were all on the other side of the choice she'd made.

With a sigh, she sat in a chair and stared at her briefcase in the corner. She'd hardly opened it since arriving, and there would be consequences for that. Perhaps now she could play catch up. Thing was, she didn't want to.

She heard the truck pull up in the driveway and pressed a hand to her stomach, inexplicably nervous. Kim was coming back to her house and Molly wanted desperately for her sister to approve of how she'd kept things. She wanted it to seem like Kim hadn't even been away. For the first time in six years, the law wasn't her first priority. Now she wasn't sure what she wanted. She had no priorities. She felt completely at sea. Without her work, what did she have? Did she have a life? Even her social life in Calgary revolved around clients and events. Then Jason had to make an appearance. Jason, who was doing exactly what he'd said he would, minus the wife and kids. Jason, who was dedicated to his work, but also dedicated to his friends and who still knew how to cut loose and enjoy the simple things, like sledding on a frosty January afternoon. Suddenly things weren't so black and white. He wasn't wrong and she wasn't right. He was all those things he'd been long ago...kind, sexy, smart. Knowing he hadn't let go of her either made the pull all that much stronger.

Molly covered her face with her hands. She'd managed to avoid the conversation he was determined to have. When he'd brought Sara home on Sunday, she'd faked a migraine so he wouldn't press. She had no idea what to say to him. Oh, why couldn't she just stop thinking? It was far too time-consuming and fatiguing.

The door opened and voices jumbled together. Molly rose from her chair, leaving her thoughts behind as she hurried to the foyer. She pasted on her cheeriest expression. "Welcome home!"

Kim looked up as she moved gingerly, taking off her jacket. Jason hung it up for her while Sara danced around her feet. Molly watched as Kim's gaze swept over the polished staircase, the tidy living room.

"Gosh, it's good to be home."

"It didn't seem right without you," Jason said, taking off his own coat then pressing a kiss to Kim's forehead. "Now you remember what the doctor said. Home but rest. Lots of it."

"Stop worrying."

"It's my job to worry about you. Don't you know that by now?" he cajoled.

"I'm not going anywhere fast, so you can stand down." Kim smiled up at Molly. "Good to see you, sis."

Molly offered a shaky smile. It was obvious that she was no substitute for Kim; Jason had as much as said so. *It didn't seem right without you.* Clearly Jason and Kim were closer than Molly had imagined. She recalled the white, strained look on his face as he described Kim's accident, then Kim's flushed cheeks later when Molly asked her about their relationship. Her eyes narrowed as her suspicions renewed. But if Jason were now hung up on her sister, he wasn't the kind of man who would try to seduce her in a laundry room. Or on a snowy hill.

Was he?

If he were as confused as she was, maybe he just would. And she'd be the woman in the middle.

"Molly? You okay?" Kim's soft voice interrupted, and Molly's feelings were suddenly overshadowed by the overwhelming relief that her sister was truly okay and back home where she belonged.

Molly waited for the crowd by the door to spread out. "Can I hug you? I don't want to pop any stitches or anything."

Kim laughed, winced, then came forward and put her arms around Molly.

Molly closed her eyes. Right now she felt closer to her sister than she had in several years. Kim had been only nineteen when Molly had left for law school. With their mother gone... Molly realized now she'd left Kim all alone to finish growing up. It was high time she made up for some of her decisions. What happened couldn't end here. She had to continue being involved in her sister's life, in Sara's life. It wasn't fair to any of them otherwise.

"I couldn't have done this without you," Kim whispered in her ear. "The house looks great, but what counts is that Sara is happy. She talked about you the whole way home. I'm so glad you came," she said, stepping back and looking Molly dead in the eye. "I don't know how to ever repay you."

Molly sniffled. "No payment necessary. We're sisters. I should have been here long ago."

"You're here now, and that's what matters."

Kim squeezed her hands, and they laughed a little with misty eyes.

Molly cleared her throat, smiling shyly. "Hang on. I'll turn on the coffee maker. We have treats."

Jason had stayed in the foyer, watching the sisters silently, but now he came forward. He knew very well from Kim that Molly hadn't visited for several years and also knew how hurt Kim had been by that. Seeing Molly acknowledge that gave him hope. Hope for her. Hope for them. He was beginning to see that Molly wasn't as cold as she'd appeared when she first arrived.

"I'll give you a hand, Mol," he offered. "Sara, why don't you and your mom go into the living room? You can show her the pictures you drew of Bubbles yesterday."

In the kitchen, he took out mugs while Molly arranged cookies and brownies on a frilly plate. She took them from a plastic container on top of the counter and not a bakery box. The woman who'd arrived a few short weeks ago would not have baked homemade goodies. His lips curved into an easy smile. She'd changed more than she realized.

"You're a good sister, Molly."

She stood back, analyzing the plate, moving a few brownies around. "No, I'm not. But I'd like to change that. Kim deserves better. We only have each other and I took that for granted."

Jason took her hand, tugging until she faced him. "I'm glad you realize that. She's very special."

A look flashed over Molly's face, and for that brief second he thought he saw distrust. But just as quickly it was gone and he was left wondering if he'd been imagining things.

Especially when she replied, "I know. And Sara should know her aunt. I've been selfish. I had intended to go back to Calgary as soon as Kim was released, but now I find I want a few more days...to make sure she can handle things, you know?"

"You did what you thought you had to do."

Her head snapped up, her gaze clashing abruptly with his. He met the look calmly. Perhaps this was what she needed to see things clearly, to finally get her priorities straight. Perhaps then....

What was it he really wanted? Molly looked away, putting away the container of cookies while a wrinkle formed between his eyebrows. Did he want her back, or did he simply want to let her go, tie up the loose ends between them and move on?

"Molly, I..."

"We'll talk later, okay? Let's just enjoy the afternoon. Kim's safe and she's home, and Sara is happy and secure again. That's what's really important. There's time enough for us to talk later."

She put the plate on a tray and he knew without a doubt what he wanted. He wanted what he'd lost six years ago.

Only now he had to figure out how he was going to make it happen.

Her hands shook as she poured a cup of milk for Sara, put everything on a tray and carried it into the living room. Sara had turned on the music channel and Kim exclaimed over the baking. Molly laughingly admitted she'd used a mix, but as they sat around the coffee table laughing and chatting, she knew she'd been missing out on something all this time.

Jason came in and took a seat, settling Sara on his lap and handing her the sippy cup of milk. Molly sat quietly, staring at the scene before her, imprinting it on her heart. To an outsider, seeing Sara on his knee, Kim's smile as she picked a brownie from the plate, they *looked* like the perfect family.

Family. People who cared about her and about each other. Ones with childhood memories and stories. That deep connection. It was no wonder Jason had gravitated to Kim. He'd always wanted a family, ever since his brother had died when he was very young. Kim was the type of homebody he needed. Yet the thought of them... Molly had to acknowledge that she wasn't willing to give him up, which was odd because he wasn't hers for the giving.

She'd forgotten how familial closeness felt. Since she'd left Jason and Kim, she'd never felt it again. They'd been her family after her parents divorced, but after him there'd been no one. Now the feeling of it rushed back, full and bittersweet with the knowledge she'd given up this place once before and that she would leave it again soon. It surprised her to realize she didn't want to. What if she were to consider the unthinkable? Was there still a place for her here? In Kim's life? In Jason's?

"Mol. Where did you go?" Kim's voice intruded and Molly forced her face to relax, conjuring a pleasant smile.

"Not far. Sorry. I'm just glad you're home."

She ignored Jason's gaze, the one that seemed to know exactly what she was thinking, and instead rose to refill the cookie plate.

How could she have forgotten?

Sara's birthday was Wednesday. Tomorrow, Molly realized. Where had the time gone? She pinched the bridge of her nose. Kim would have had a party all arranged long before now, complete with presents and cake and probably a half dozen children running around. Kim was home, yes, but still on pain killers, still exhausted. And as nice as it was for Sara to have her mommy back, things were far from normal in that household.

Sara was turning four. Molly had missed enough birthdays that she was determined to make up for it. Kim and Sara were the only family she had left and so far she hadn't even made an effort. That was going to change. Starting today.

When Kim had mentioned it this morning, asking Molly if she could run out and pick up at least a few presents, Molly had known that wouldn't be enough. Besides, Kim had been off work for nearly three weeks. She was a single parent. Molly didn't have to read too closely between the lines to know that money was tight for her baby sister. To make up for past neglect, Molly was determined to make this birthday one to remember.

"I'll look after it, I promise," Molly assured her. "You get up some strength for a little party, okay?"

Except Molly had no idea how to organize a child's party.

She and Jason hadn't talked about what was happening between them since that kiss in the snow, and Molly knew they had to clear the air. Asking him for help would be awkward, yet she couldn't think of anyone else to help with the party. She'd already decided against having extra children. She knew her limits and also knew Kim didn't need that much commotion. It would be a family event. No one knew Kim and Sara better than Jason, so that afternoon Molly swallowed her anxiety and misgivings and stopped at the clinic.

Jason turned a corner and saw her there, waiting patiently for him, looking fresh and beautiful in snug jeans and Kim's puffy pink bomber jacket, a scarf twisted around her neck. When she turned from the window to face him, sunlight backlit her golden hair and her eyes, normally a placid blue, glowed pale and bright.

She was his angel. Always had been, always would be. Ten years ago now, he'd fallen for her, and nothing had changed. But he'd been burned badly enough by her before that there was no way he'd let her see that. Not yet. Not until she came to him. He wouldn't put himself out there and bare his soul only to have it thrown back at him again. But if he could get her to make the first move...

"Molly. What's up? Is something wrong? Kim and Sara all right?"

"Everyone's fine. Have you got a sec?"

"I've got ten minutes before my next client." He didn't mention that there were a zillion things he could be doing in that ten minutes. He had precious few moments with Molly left, and for once, work could wait. If she was going to come to him, he had to give her reason to.

He led her back past the exam rooms to the tiny cubbyhole that housed a fridge and a single set of cupboards. "Want a drink?"

"No, thanks," she said, pulling a stool up to the counter.

"Mind if I do? I don't often get an opportunity for a break."

"Go ahead."

He grabbed a can of soda from the fridge and sat opposite her, popping the top. "So what's up?"

"I have a problem."

"Shoot."

"Sara's birthday is tomorrow."

"I know. I've had her present for a month."

Molly laughed. "Why am I not surprised? I, however, do not, and neither does Kim. I want to have a birthday party. Just the family, though. But I don't know much about children her age. Everything I know is based on the last few weeks. I don't even know where to start and her birthday is tomorrow."

"You want me to help." He grinned at her. Shopping for Sara was fun. Doing it with Molly was exactly what the doctor ordered. It was as good an excuse as any to spend time with her. Even better was that she'd done the suggesting. She couldn't accuse him of coming up with ways to keep them together.

"Yes, I'm asking for your help. You know both of them better than I do. Though it pains me to admit it."

He ignored the last bit; it would be nice to have a conversation without an argument or recriminations being bandied back and forth. "I'm done here at six. We can hit the mall."

"Thank you. I think Kim's finances are...well, tight, and I'd like to make up for that."

"You can afford to?" He offered it as a question, raising an eyebrow, rather than a statement. Molly had done what she'd said she would. She'd become successful. It was high time she realized that she had a family and he was pleased she was taking the initiative. If she wanted to spend a little of that money on making Sara's birthday special, he had no problem helping. It also would be a good chance for him to see if he was right about her...that she'd changed and cared more about her family than about her career and her gold card.

"My salary's substantial, yes." She blushed a bit. "And I've only had myself to support. Besides that, Sara's had a rough time and she's been so good through it all. It's the least I can do."

Jason reached over and clasped her hand. Molly probably didn't even realize it, but he'd seen changes in her over the past few weeks. When she'd arrived, she'd had this veneer around her, protecting her from feeling too much. He'd seen it the moment he'd opened the door. Yet bit by bit she'd relaxed. The designer clothes had been replaced with pieces of Kim's more comfortable wardrobe. She'd expected less of Sara and had enjoyed more. Her cold manner had dissipated completely when he'd held her in his arms. It would be very easy to fall in love with her again. And very hard not to show her how he was feeling. But first and foremost he had to protect his heart. If things changed, they had to be on his terms. It was the only way he could keep himself from being hurt.

"I'm glad you've realized how special they are," he murmured, squeezing her fingers. "I'll pick you up."

His client was waiting, so he merely rose, dropped a fleeting kiss on the crest of her cheek and disappeared into an exam room. Oh yes, Molly held more power than she could possibly know. He'd tried, but no one in the intervening years had ever measured up. Now that she was back, he wasn't sure he could risk that kind of heartbreak again. He had to be sure of her first.

They hit the toy store first. One stop shopping, Jason had said, and as Molly pushed the cart and Jason filled it up, her eyes grew larger and larger with the amount of loot that piled up.

"Do you have a theme?"

"A theme?"

He laughed as they halted before the party supplies. "You know, what kind of plates, napkins, balloons, that sort of thing."

Molly looked over the selection, which covered an entire wall. "How about princesses or something?"

"That sounds about right." He leaned over to pick out plates, napkins and cups in pink and pale blue, and his scrubs stretched taut. Molly's mouth watered. All the reasons she'd left so long ago faded into the distant past. Instead she was reminded of how he'd kissed her in the snow, how he'd held her hand this afternoon. She'd thought perhaps parting as friends would be easier, leaving the bitterness behind. But it wasn't going to be easier at all. Molly knew leaving Jason, after all that had transpired, was going to hurt all over again. And this time she wouldn't have righteous indignation to pull her through. If she came back again, they'd have to find a way to make peace with the past so they could move forward. Talk about a gigantic task. She laughed inwardly at herself. She never had been one to take the easy road.

He put the items in the cart and looked up at her when she didn't follow along. "Are you coming?"

She nodded. "Sorry. Preoccupied."

"What did Kim want to get her?"

They started down another aisle, one completely pink. Didn't girl's things come in any other color?

"She said something about a play kitchen. But I don't know what kind."

She really was horrible. She didn't even know how to shop for a little girl, for goodness sake! She had to refer to a single man for shopping advice!

"Here they are." Jason halted in front of a display. "Which one do you like best?"

She stared at the selection. "I don't know. I'm hopeless at this sort of thing."

Jason leaned over. "You were four once. What would you have wanted?"

Molly stared at the different designs, her heart heavy. "You know better than to ask that, Jason," she murmured. She could feel him looking at her and refused to meet his gaze.

"I'm sorry, Molly," he said softly from behind her. "I never thought."

What he'd done with that one simple question was stir up old memories she had no desire to recall. She looked at the toys. Plastic or wood. Pink and white or tan and green. Ironing boards or dishwashers. So many choices in miniature and she knew that not once in her life had she had toys such as these. She understood Kim wanting to have things for Sara that they'd never had. Their own parents had divorced when they were young and their mother had all but abandoned them when they finished high school, remarrying and moving away.

There'd been many things they'd wanted for as children—not only the presents but the thought and love that went behind the gifts. Feeling treasured. That was what had drawn her to Jason in the first place. He'd understood that need, as he'd felt it himself. The warm family he'd known had faded away after his brother Jonathan's death. Molly and Jason had become fiercely independent, thinking they didn't need those things. Kim had been younger and had handled things differently. For the first time, Molly faced the fact that she'd done the same thing as her mother—run away. She'd handled the neglect in one way, Kim the polar opposite. She'd put a wall around her heart; Kim had become the giving nurturer. It was obvious which one Jason truly needed. It was understandable.

Kim was trying desperately to give her daughter a sense of family, all on her own. Kim was the one who had always realized what family meant even in the absence of it, had always been the nurturing one even though Molly had been oldest. Molly looked up and saw the biggest, most elaborate item and pointed. "That one. The one with all the bells and whistles."

Jason stared at it, his eyes flicking to the price tag. "It's a bit expensive, don't you think?"

"I'll cover it. Kim can accept this bit of help, just this once."

Jason picked up the tag. "It's too big. We'll have to give them this at the register and have it brought out."

Molly smiled then. The glee in the fact that the present was so big made her feel silly and childish, and she liked it. She had money and couldn't think of a better way to use it than putting a smile on her niece's face.

"We need accessories."

They went down another aisle, Molly fighting the feeling that she and Jason were shopping for their own child. If they'd stayed together, they very well could have had a child Sara's age. She shook off the feeling. Sara wasn't their child, and she and Jason weren't a couple. They were simply shopping for her niece's birthday.

She picked out a porcelain tea set in white with pink roses sprayed on the cups. She added a child's size cobbler's apron and a plastic carry bag of play food, so Sara's playtime with her new kitchen would be complete.

At the cash register she never batted an eyelash at the total, just took out her credit card, signed the slip and headed for the truck with Jason carrying the bags.

They were followed out by an attendant who helped load the huge box in the back.

"Now we need a cake."

Jason laughed. "Of course."

Molly checked her watch. "Is anything even still open?"

"Yeah. The grocery's open twenty-four hours."

Walking into the brightly lit store, it felt somewhat like a ghost town. Only a handful of shoppers wandered the quiet aisles. At the bakery counter, they ordered a cake to pick up the following day and made their way to the frozen section to pick up party food.

She was putting animal shaped chicken nuggets in the cart when Jason's voice came quietly behind her.

"Do you feel it, too?"

His words washed over her, soft and wistful, and she knew exactly what he meant. Did it feel strange to be shopping for a cake and presents for a blonde bombshell with curly hair and dark intelligent eyes so much like his?

"A little." She kept her back to him. Looking at him now wouldn't be wise. She'd forget everything she desperately needed to remember. Like how she couldn't afford for fantasy to take over common sense.

"It could have been us."

Tears pricked her eyes as he put words to her earlier thoughts. So easily, if she'd followed in line with his plan. They could be celebrating their own little girl's birthday, shopping together. But that had been the problem. He'd planned everything down to the last detail, and she hadn't been ready for that. Now the chance had passed them by, and she did feel the pain of the death of that dream warring with the frightening prospect of hope that all hadn't been lost.

"Do you ever wonder?" he continued, close behind her. She could feel his body even though he never touched her.

In the end, fear won.

She took a fortifying breath and lied. "No. I'm not the kind of person who dwells on what might have been."

She felt his withdrawal in response to her icy words. The air cooled behind her and relief mixed with regret. He was making it harder and harder to leave, and she couldn't forget that if she let him, he'd try to order her life all over again. He still didn't see that what he'd done was wrong. He was still sure he was right and that she'd been wrong to run. They were both forgetting that and letting the nostalgia of the good things between them distract them from the big problem. A problem that wouldn't disappear no matter where she lived. The one thing they hadn't discussed since being home.

It was one thing to remember the past. It was another to forget exactly why she'd left in the first place.

"We'd better get going." She turned the cart toward the checkout, heard his footsteps behind her but didn't dare meet his eyes.

She didn't want him to know how much the lie had cost her.

CHAPTER EIGHT

Jason took Sara to the clinic with him the next afternoon, giving Molly time to prepare for the party. Molly went to work hanging streamers and a huge pink and white sign that had "Happy Birthday" emblazoned on it. The party was set for the kitchen. It would certainly be easier to clean up chocolate fudge cake with bright pink icing from the kitchen floor than the thick living room carpet.

The dishes were placed on top of a white-and-pink paper tablecloth. Various princesses danced across it and the pattern was repeated on the paper plates, cups and napkins. Balloons had been delivered and were arranged around the room. Molly moved the cake in its plastic domed carton, hiding it behind the set of canisters and away from Sara's keen eyes. She was nervous, of all things. Nervous at what Jason would think of what she'd done. Hoping it was good enough.

She couldn't blame him for thinking her cold and uncaring. From the moment she'd refused his ring, she hadn't given him a reason to believe her anything different. He didn't know all the fears, the uncertainty. He knew how lonely she'd been. All her life she'd longed for love. But he didn't know that when it finally had happened, she'd let it swallow her up until she'd almost lost herself. She'd loved him so much that she'd almost let herself be assimilated into his ultimate life-plan. Leaving him had been a rebellious act of desperation to try to stay in one piece. She'd distanced herself from even her sister, the only one who might understand, in order to protect her heart.

Now that she was home, seeing a glimpse of their past, the poignancy of the present and the seriousness of Kim's condition... She knew she'd been utterly wrong. Perhaps not in breaking things off—Jason *had* been terribly heavy-handed—but she'd been wrong to run away and not deal with him. Wrong to stay far away from Kim and Sara. She was trying hard to make up for it. Today felt like a test, and knowing it was the time to find out if she'd pass or fail made her tummy twine up in tangly knots.

Molly turned her head toward the ceiling as she heard Kim running the bathtub. Why was it so hard to resist the memories? Why couldn't Jason have gotten fat and bald over the years, instead of becoming even more mouth-wateringly handsome? She put her head in her hands. It was time to face the truth, if only to herself. She'd never stopped loving him. It sounded easy, but was so very hard. She loved him for all the things that hadn't changed, yet the reasons she left in the first place were still there. He would still expect her to be the one to do all the giving up. It wasn't that she wasn't willing to sacrifice. She always had been willing to compromise. It was knowing he would *expect* her to while he kept his life the same, knowing he'd have everything pigeon-holed in a cookie-cutter existence that still had her balking.

For even if she were tempted to leave her life behind and start anew, she knew that if she did, she'd resent him for it sooner or later.

When the phone rang she jumped, then swiveled to grab the cordless unit. Minutes later when she hung up, her hands shook and her stomach quivered.

Her decision had just gotten that much harder.

Jason returned with Sara at five o'clock sharp. In his right hand, he held a bag containing a change of clothes, and in the other was a large box wrapped in birthday paper. Sara rang the doorbell and giggled at her mother, who opened the door wearing a pink party hat.

"You take this." He handed Kim the present. "I'm going to get changed first."

"Sure, go ahead. We're just getting supper on."

He changed from his scrubs to jeans and a sweater and ran a hand through his hair.

He didn't have much time left, he knew it. Molly's trip was nearly over and she'd be going back to Calgary unless he took some drastic action. But he wasn't sure what that action should be. He'd tried to talk to her last night about the feelings that had run between them. He'd known she was thinking about what might have been. He'd sensed it, because he'd been feeling it, too. Maybe if they could start talking about how good things had been... But after he'd mentioned it, she'd shut him out completely. Shaking his head, he stuffed his dirty scrubs into the bag. Perhaps he *should* let her go. Maybe it would be easier for everyone that way. It was certainly long past time.

When he entered the kitchen, Sara was wearing her princess tiara and looking very regal in her favourite pink fairy dress, the layers of tulle puffing about her. Molly was taking a cookie sheet out of the oven and Kim overturned the deep fryer basket, dumping chicken nuggets on to a plate lined with paper towel.

"Hey, girls," he said from the doorway, and Molly spun, her hands still encased in blue oven mitts and holding the pan.

"Feel better?" Kim spoke into the breach of silence that fell. Molly turned to get a spatula for the potato smiley faces, but not before Jason saw the fleeting expression of consternation on her face. She was isolating herself. And somehow he sensed it had nothing to do with last night.

"Need some help?" he offered lightly, taking the plate from Kim. Molly still avoided his glance as she filled a bowl with the potato shapes.

"We're good," Kim answered cryptically, but he could see by her overly bright smile that she knew exactly what was going on and dread curled around, dark and unknown, in his stomach. Something was wrong.

Sara's chatter at the table made up for the lack of conversation, but Jason watched Molly closely. Her mouth was thin and unhappy, her eyes weary. Once she met Kim's eyes and he knew that whatever it was, Molly had confided in her sister. He was clearly out of the loop.

"So what's first, muffin?" He forced his tone to be light and happy for Sara's sake. "Presents or cake?"

Sara pushed away her plate, leaving half a nugget stuck in the circle of ketchup. "Presents! Presents!"

He laughed. "You got it." Disappearing around the corner, he brought out his present to her. She tore at the pink paper, giving an excited squeal as he helped her open the box.

Inside was a puppet show. Taking off the plastic wrap, he showed her how to fold back the sides so it would stand alone, tie back the curtains with Velcro and open the bag of finger puppets inside. Eyes wide, she put on a lion and zebra while he donned a monkey and they acted out, wiggling their fingers and talking in sometimes high, sometimes growly, animal-ish voices.

"Do you like it?"

"I love it! Thanks, Uncle Jason."

"You're welcome. Let's see what your mama got you."

Kim stayed in her seat, her face drawn and pale from the unaccustomed excitement while Jason put away the puppet show and motioned for Molly to help him with the toy kitchen. Together they went to the basement and carried up the assembled toy, the silence between them awkward as Molly avoided his gaze again.

"Shut your eyes," he called from the hall, and they brought it into the kitchen, a huge pink bow on the top of the cupboard.

"Okay, you can open them now."

Sara's eyes were as wide as silver dollars as she stared at the miniature kitchen with her mouth open. It was taller than she was and twice as wide. Sliding off her chair, she reached out a disbelieving hand, touching the sink and the play toaster. "Ohhhh, Mommy," she whispered, and Jason looked over at Kim.

Tears had gathered in her Kim's eyes and she held her fingers over her mouth. Tearing her gaze from her daughter she looked up at Jason and Molly. "Thank you," she whispered as Sara moved from spot to spot, trying it out. "I know what I gave you didn't cover it."

"We wanted to," Molly answered with a warm smile.

"Mommy, it's just what I wanted!" The initial shock had worn off and Sara started to bounce. "Look! A dishwasher and fridge and oven and everything!"

Jason laughed at the girl's ebullience, but laid assessing eyes on Molly. She'd given Kim credit for the gift, even though she had helped pay for it. Her smile broadened at the approval that had come from Kim. His brow wrinkled thoughtfully, listening to Sara's chatter in the background, thanking her aunt for picking it out. Perhaps Molly *had* changed. Because it was clear to him that she was trying to make up in the only way she knew how for not being here. But soon she'd be gone and he knew that presents didn't make up for a lack of love. He wasn't sure Molly understood that yet.

"Sara, I think your Aunt Molly got you something, too," Kim's voice intruded.

"You did?"

Molly smiled. "Yes, I did. It's in the living room."

Sara rushed out, sliding back over the floor with the pink box in hand. Hurriedly she ripped off the paper and opened up the accessories to her kitchen.

"Oh, thank you, Aunt Molly!" Impulsively Sara rocketed over to give Molly a genuine hug, looping her arms around her aunt's neck and kissing her cheek. Molly's lips were frozen in a permanent smile. "This is the best birthday *ever!*"

Everyone laughed, contented to watch as Sara donned her apron and set about making everyone tea to go with their birthday cake.

While Kim was putting candles on the cake, Jason rose and laid a hand on Molly's shoulder as they watched Sara playing. He leaned close to her ear. "So Molly saves the day," he murmured, and although he didn't hear it, he sensed the frustrated sigh coming from within her.

"I certainly didn't intend to," she hissed back. "Just save it, okay? I'm not in the mood right now."

He flattened his chin at her sharp reply, taken aback when he'd only been teasing. "I wasn't meaning to be critical," he defended. Whatever was bothering her, it had to be something big to put her this much on edge. "Are you okay?" His voice was low with concern he couldn't help but feel even in his disappointment. He knelt before her chair and looked up at her.

Her eyes were tortured, and he only remembered one other time he'd seen her so inwardly torn up about anything. The day he'd asked her to marry him and she'd refused. His chest was heavy and weighted as tears gleamed in her eyes and she averted her head and tried to blink them away. Her expression, her anguish, reached out to him, so tangible he felt it without even knowing the cause. Yet what could be this big to tear her up inside so very much?

"Honey, what's wrong?" Worry had the endearment slipping out without him even thinking about it.

At that moment, Kim rounded the corner with the cake, candles lit and singing "Happy Birthday". He tore his gaze from Molly's for a moment and when he turned back, she'd replaced her expression with one of bleak enthusiasm for Sara's sake. The little princess perched on her chair while they all sang and she blew out her candles.

He didn't get a chance to talk to Molly again until Kim took a very tired birthday girl upstairs to put on her pajamas. Molly was scraping dishes and loading the dishwasher, the light above the sink the only glow in the dark room. "Molly."

Her hand paused for a moment, then put a teacup in the top rack.

He stopped her with a hand on her arm. "Are you going to tell me what's wrong now?"

She sighed, a heavy exhalation of exhaustion and annoyance. "I don't want to do this now, okay? Let it go."

He turned her away from the dishwasher and looked her square in the eye. "If I did something to tick you off, I want to know."

Her smile was grim. "You didn't do anything. You've been great. Even when you were judging me earlier."

He didn't know how to answer, so he kept his lips closed.

"You're not denying it. Well, at least I read that right. Don't worry, Jason. This has nothing to do with you, not directly."

"Then why the tears? Why are you unhappy?" *Please, come to me,* he thought. It had been hard enough to accept the fact that he still had feelings for her. She had to be the one to turn to him first.

Giggles erupted from upstairs and they both looked at the ceiling. When their gazes met again, Molly set her lips, erecting an icy barrier between them.

"Say goodnight to Sara, Jason. I need to talk to you, but not here, not now. Once the mess is cleaned up, I'll come over. I promise."

"You sound like you're going to your own execution."

She tried a laugh but fell flat. "Maybe. Just go home."

Her tone was so weary, so defeated, he agreed. "I'll wait up for you."

She nodded, and before he could give in and kiss her like he wanted to, he headed for the stairs to say his goodbyes.

Jason entered his house, disturbed by how quiet it was after the chaos of next door. This was the time of day he hated the most...coming home to an empty, quiet house. Growing up he'd loved having his family together, laughing, talking, arguing. When his little brother had died, Jason had been eight years old, and suddenly the house had been quiet and solemn all the time. But then Uncle Jim and Aunt Susan and their kids had come to live with them for a while, and the house had seemed to fill with laughter and confusion again. By the time they'd left, his parents had been better able to cope with having only one child, and he'd been close with them always. He missed them still, but understood why they'd chosen to retire somewhere else. They visited when they could, but Jason knew the real way to get them to visit more often was to give them a reason—such as a daughter-in-law and a couple of grandkids.

He slumped on to the sofa. That had been the plan, but he was no closer to it now than he'd been six years ago when Molly had walked out on him.

It had been good before that. Why did she have to come back after all these years and stir up all the old memories? When she'd first arrived, their meetings had been about anger and regret. Somehow now, the anger had gone, and he was reminded of all the reasons he'd loved her to begin with. The more she was here, the more he saw glimpses of the old Molly, the girl he'd loved so much he'd wanted to spend the rest of his life with her.

Seeing the devastated look in her eyes at the party, knowing she would be coming over later, had put him in the frame of mind to be nostalgic. To recall the good times, not the fights or the bad ending. He grabbed a lighter and lit a few candles around the living room, turned on the CD player and, with a long held sigh, dropped to the couch.

He swallowed. He'd loved her completely. Why had he ever thought he could put that aside with anger as his weapon? All he'd done was hide behind the anger, denying the truth and never dealing with it.

Wax was dripping lazily from the candles when he heard the door open then shut again with a quiet click. He didn't even bother to try to hide his melancholy mood. Perhaps now she deserved to know how very deeply she'd hurt him, how much he'd loved her. Perhaps now she needed to see the real results from her walking away. Perhaps it wasn't about who would make the first move forward, but who would make the first one to deal with the fallout of the past.

She stopped in the doorway, and he saw indecision flicker in her eyes. "What are you doing?"

He smiled up at her. "Remembering."

She took a few more steps in. "Remembering what?"

"The way we used to love each other."

Molly felt her heart give two solid thumps and her hands began to shake. Not now. This was going to be hard enough without him getting all sentimental on her. Someone here had to keep a clear and unemotional head. She'd been hoping it wouldn't have to be her.

"That was a long time ago," she chided.

But he patted the cushion beside him. "Come, sit," he suggested gently.

Impatience and anger flared up seemingly out of nowhere. Sweet talking was *not* what she needed right now. What she needed was to stop tip-toeing around the past, stop being stupidly emotional and just *deal.*

"The people we were then thought they could have everything. We both know that life isn't like that." Her tone was cold and flat as she systematically started to shut down her feelings.

Molly couldn't read his expression at her words and avoided looking into his eyes. She knew if she got caught up in the moment, she'd lose her nerve to say what she'd come to say.

"I came to tell you I'm leaving tomorrow," Molly said abruptly.

"Tomorrow?" The hands that had been calm suddenly raked through his hair. "But you weren't supposed to leave until Sunday."

"Do three more days make that much difference?" She looked up at him then and put her hands in her pockets to keep from reaching out and smoothing his hair away from his face. "I got called back now. I have to go."

"Your job? This is about work?"

She missed the threatening note in his question. Fact was, she was undeniably angry at the ultimatum her boss had delivered this afternoon. Sure, she'd been distracted while here and she hadn't exactly kept up with her files. She knew that, but she had planned to put in extra time once she got back to Calgary, getting things in order so there'd be less fuss when she did something she never thought she'd do. Put in her notice. After all, time was all she was going to have, wasn't it? But instead she'd gotten *the call* today, reaming her out for neglecting an important client, *demanding* she return immediately or face consequences. Hearing her boss's voice on the phone, making demands, told her she was making the right choice in walking away. She wanted more, something better where she could be happy and make a difference. Kim was home and doing well. Jason was next door if they needed anything. Why did leaving feel so very wrong? Why did she resent it so much?

The answer came swiftly—because once again, the choice was being taken out of her hands.

"I let things slide. I have to go make things right." She ached to tell him she'd be returning to Fredericton, but something in his closed expression held her back. She got the slippery feeling he was judging her again and making this decision had been hard enough without him weighing in on it.

To her surprise, Jason snorted. "Nice boss. Doesn't even give you three weeks' vacation."

"Look," she defended, "I told them I'd work from here. But I got behind, didn't follow through. I have to go back to finish what I started."

Silence. Her last sentence echoed through the room, and mingled with the soft sounds coming from the stereo. In that heavy silence, they both heard the truth—she had never been too concerned with going back and making things right before.

But she was here, now, to change that. Things needed to be said before she left. Things left far too long to fester and hurt. At least this time when she left he'd know exactly why.

"Leaving again. So do you plan on buying your sister's and niece's affection every now and then to salve your conscience?" His words came out in bitter staccato.

"You know that's not what I did. You can't buy someone's love. I was trying to help, to make up for the times I haven't been here. They both deserve that."

That crease appeared between his brows again. "The Molly that arrived here three weeks ago would have thrown her money around for effect."

She eyed him curiously. "She probably would have. But I'm not the same person I was when I arrived. Thank goodness."

She took a step forward, stopping before she got close enough to touch him. "I didn't say goodbye to you before, Jason, and...and I'm sorry. But I'm saying it this time."

She perched on the arm of a chair, stared into the flickering flames of the gas fireplace. He'd known she was coming over and he'd deliberately set up the scene with candles and music. But the truth was they were not the same people they'd been. A romantic setting wouldn't change all there was—and wasn't—between them. Again she questioned her decision to come back here permanently. Would it be too hard with Jason as a constant reminder? Would it keep them from moving on after all? Would it be better to find a whole new place for a new beginning?

"Why didn't you say goodbye? Why did you leave the way you did?"

The answer was easy enough, and now was the time for truth. "Because I was angry. Because I still loved you and I felt like I'd be beating my head against a brick wall trying to make you understand how I felt. And because..." Her throat closed against the threat of tears. The years they'd shared deserved the truth, however late it was in coming. "Because I was afraid you'd be able to convince me to stay."

His gaze snapped to hers in surprise. She wished he would stop looking at her that way. He had the most beautiful, penetrating eyes of any man she'd ever known, with the uncanny ability to make her feel as if he could see right into her soul. Right now she did not want him to see that deeply inside her.

"I would have had that power?"

She took a breath. "Yeah. You would have. And I couldn't let that happen, because I knew—I *know*—that I would have ended up hating you for it in the end."

"I loved you."

"I know you did. That's why it hurt so much, don't you see?" She rose from the chair and went to the fireplace, resting her hands on the mantle. "I knew that you loved me, and even when I felt I was right making the decision I did, I still felt I was wrong for hurting you. I couldn't handle it, so I left. I was determined to build the life *I* wanted. To show you I'd been right."

"But..."

She turned, tears glimmering on her lashes. "But being right cost me. I didn't realize until lately how very much I'd given up by leaving."

"What did you give up, Molly?" His voice came across the room huskily.

Her gaze delved deeply into his.

"Everything," she admitted.

The room fell quiet as the music stopped, then with a whirring sound switched to the next CD. When the piano notes started, Molly's heart leapt, constricted and cracked, and the tears on her lashes spilled on to her cheeks.

Jason stood, took agonizingly slow steps to her as the introduction ended and the vocals began to *their* song. He reached out and took her hand, saying softly, "Dance with me."

Helpless to refuse, she curled her fingers in his and let him draw her close as their feet made tiny circles to the music. The words, which years ago had seemed so different, now seemed crafted to their own unique, twisted situation, each syllable branding a bit more pain on Molly's already hurting heart. His body fit against hers perfectly, even after all these years. He pulled her closer, closer, so close she could feel his heart beating against her.

"Are you listening, Molly?"

She swallowed. She had no idea how many times they'd danced to this song in years past, but never had it had such a poignant meaning as now. Now it was about finding love again after years apart, of how empty life had been until they'd found each other again, the singer was begging *her* to stay. Did Jason want her still? Did he want her to stay with him, to give their love another chance?

"I'm listening," she whispered as his hand trailed intimately down her back, sliding over her hip and making every nerve ending in her body stand to order.

"Then tell me," he murmured, his voice soft but tight with emotion.

"I can't," she whispered painfully.

His lips nuzzled at her ear and she forgot the plane ticket in her purse, forgot she was supposed to be saying goodbye, and simply leaned her head back and met his lips with hers. Of all the kisses they'd shared since she'd returned, this one undid her. This one, a kiss that was a hello, a reunion, an acknowledgement. Somehow, in some way they'd both admitted that their love had never died, and this was the ultimate manifestation of those feelings. Molly couldn't say the words; she was too afraid. But she poured all her emotions into that kiss—her regret, her sadness, her love.

The song ended but the kiss lingered, turning into a series of nips and brief contacts that trailed down her neck. "Stay," he whispered against the column of her throat. "Stay with me tonight."

Could she? Could she stay, knowing she would be leaving tomorrow?

It was impossible to be rational when his fingers were caressing the small of her back. "That probably wouldn't be a good idea."

"Probably not." He whispered the words next to her ear. "But life is full of bad ideas."

One last chance. This would be the one and only time she'd have to touch him, love him the way she'd missed loving him. *This could be the sweet goodbye they'd missed.*

Or it could break her heart.

He straightened, put a finger under her chin and lifted it until she looked him in the eyes. "I've asked you to stay. I want to make love to you. But the decision is yours, Molly."

She lifted a shaky hand to his cheek, smiled a wobbly smile.

"Love me one last time, Jason."

CHAPTER NINE

His eyes blazed at her words. Saying nothing, he reached out and began unfastening her blouse button by torturous button. Once he was done, he pushed it from her shoulders, his gaze lighting on her pale skin. It was as tangible as a caress. Molly's breath shook as she exhaled, reached for his sweater and tugged at the hem.

He helped her pull it over his head, dropping it on the floor beside her blouse. Hesitantly she reached out and touched his chest—*like this?*—her fingertips asked. His palm covered her breast possessively. *Like this.*

Molly moved closer, running both hands over his skin now, the warm, smooth expanse of his chest, the strong curves of his arms. She worried the waistband of his jeans with her fingernails, pulling him close. Their torsos touched, warm, magnetic, and she knew nothing in the world had ever felt as right as his skin pressed against hers.

The CD changed again, to something soft and bluesy while the firelight flickered around them, creating light and shadow. Molly touched her lips to the hollow between his shoulder and collarbone, tasting the saltiness there with the tip of her tongue, hearing the sharp intake of breath in his lungs. Her tongue slid from that hollow down to flick over his nipple, and he groaned.

Drawing her back up for a hot, open-mouthed kiss, he trailed his right hand down her back to release the clasp of her bra and blindly slid it off her arms.

It was like before but better, familiar yet new as he took her hand and led her to the fireplace. He grabbed a green throw from the sofa and laid it over the braided rug, tossing a few cushions after it. Seeing it— a nest, the place where she'd be one with him again— almost made her change her mind. But then he smiled, soft, knowing, and she knew there was nothing she wanted more than to be with him. She unfastened her jeans, slid them down over her legs and left them laying on the floor beside the rug.

"You're more beautiful now than you were then," he said huskily, shaking his head. "I didn't think that was possible."

"Things change."

"Some things don't."

She padded over to him on bare feet. When had she ever been this comfortable with a man? Certainly not since she'd left *him.* She was standing in the dusky light in nothing but a pair of tiny white panties and she didn't feel the least bit of discomfort or awkwardness. From their first time it had been like this. All she felt now was anticipation. Because she *knew.* Knew what was in store.

"You're a bit overdressed, don't you think?" Her voice came out as a teasing sing-song and she couldn't hold back the sexy laugh that escaped as his eyes widened. She unbuttoned his jeans and pushed them down over his lean hips, taking his briefs with them. When they were gone, she reached for him.

"The blanket," he muttered hoarsely in her ear seconds later. "The blanket, or so help me God I'm not going to be able to stand."

She lay down on the blanket, her hair spread on the pillows, invitation clear. When he knelt beside her, his gaze never leaving hers, she knew she was in trouble. Glorious, bone-melting trouble.

This wasn't one last time, not for her. She loved him again, heart and soul. Tomorrow was going to break her heart, but tonight...tonight would be the parting memory she'd take with her. Something much more beautiful than the bitter words six years ago. A celebration of the love they'd once shared.

His fingers slid along the inside of her thigh and she quivered. "Touch me," she whispered, moaning when he answered her command.

His lips covered hers, swallowing her groan. When she thought she couldn't possibly go another moment without breath, he pulled away and dropped kisses on her neck, her collarbone, her breasts. He pulled a taut nipple into his mouth and she arched, her body a perfect bow. Between his hands and his lips right now she was a quivering pool of sensations, all of her senses attuned to him. The way he smelled. The way his skin rubbed against hers. The sound of his breathing, heavy and aroused. The contrast of his dark hair against the creamy skin of her breasts. How could she possibly have forgotten how good this was?

Pulling away, he inched her panties down her legs until they were gone. When he covered her body with his she lost all perspective and guided him inside her, arching to meet him.

The sound of their breathing mingled with the music, pulsing through her like a throbbing heartbeat. Molly's eyes stung with unshed tears as she realized she didn't want this to be an end. She wanted a beginning. She loved him more now, if that were possible, and felt helpless to tell him. She would try in every way to show him, right now.

She put her hands on his hips, slowing the movements, drawing them out. "Love me," she whispered, sliding a fingernail over the curve of his hip.

He stilled. She felt their contact, their link, as if everything in their bodies was centered on that one perfect point of union. When she thought she couldn't possibly bear it any more, he whispered in her ear.

"I do." And he started moving again, taking her up, up, and she met his hips equally, watching the glow of the flames flicker over his skin, seeing them dance in his eyes.

"Like this?" he murmured, twisting his hips and making her cry out.

"Mmmmmm," was all she could manage, trying desperately to maintain the fragile thread of control.

His voice became a growl. "Like *this*," he confirmed, twisting again and she gave up, gripping his shoulders with her fingers while she shattered beneath him.

He held on, took her over and followed with a final thrust so powerful it slid the rug six inches up the hardwood floor.

Molly turned her head towards the fire so Jason wouldn't see the tears in her eyes. She'd done this to feel whole again. To remember and take with her the sweet memory of loving Jason Elliot. Instead she felt only the emptiness of defeat. She had to leave tomorrow. But the simple fact was Jason wasn't trying to convince her to stay. He was accepting her leaving and not even fighting for her. He was doing what she'd thought she wanted—letting her go.

He curled up behind her, covering her thigh with his, warming her skin now that the heated blood-rush of lovemaking was waning. Molly knew that to say anything at all would betray her emotions. She remained quiet, listening to his breathing at her shoulder.

Warmed by the fire, she fell asleep there. And woke an hour later.

She'd been asleep in Jason's arms. Three weeks ago if she'd been told that she'd be sleeping with Jason again, she would have said, "Not in this lifetime!" But here she was, in a bigger mess than she'd been before.

Nothing had changed. She was still leaving; it was still over. What they'd shared had been nothing more than a beautiful goodbye.

Molly closed her eyes, taking a few moments to imprint the feeling of being in his arms on her heart. She slid out from their warmth, retrieved her underwear. As she dressed, she watched him sleep— his lips relaxed, his eyelashes on his cheeks. The beautiful form of him on the blanket. He had been hers. Tonight she had been reminded of all she'd thrown away... All it would have taken even all those years ago was for him to compromise, just a little. To let go of all the *plans* and just let them *be*. But he hadn't. And he wouldn't. So she buttoned her blouse and prepared to leave.

"Going somewhere?"

The husky note in his voice stopped her at the door to the living room. She answered without looking at him.

"I should get back to Kim's. I haven't finished packing, and my flight leaves early."

"At least look at me, Mol."

She heard rather than saw him rise up to sitting on the blanket behind her, and felt his stare burrowing into the back of her head. She closed her eyes against the knowledge that what she'd said had sounded cold.

She turned, slowly, met his gaze.

"I don't want you to go yet," he said.

She sighed. She couldn't let herself feel hope at his words. She'd been broken enough over him before. But hope...hope always ended badly. Something always happened to disappoint and then all that was left was to pick up the pieces.

"We're only prolonging the inevitable. My flight does leave tomorrow; we can't pretend that it doesn't."

Jason crossed his arms over his knees. "That doesn't mean you have to be on it."

"What do you mean?"

"Stay."

She waited, willing him with all her heart to say the *right* words this time.

"Stay with me tonight, Molly. Come to my bed, make love to me again. Let me change your mind."

Molly froze.

Let me change your mind. Those words echoed through her, stretching back six long, lonely years. This had been her greatest fear. And now, in the aftermath of their lovemaking, he had the power to do it all again.

He couldn't realize that those had been the exact words he'd used that June morning. As if somehow she'd come around to the way he wanted things.

"Don't. Don't do this to me again."

The line between his eyebrows wrinkled in confusion. "What exactly just happened? What am I doing again?"

He rose, grabbed his pants and pulled them on, leaving them unbuttoned.

Panic threaded through her. "Persuasion, that's what!" She took another two steps backward, putting distance between them. "What's your plan this time, Jason? Make love to me until I'm a puddle of goo, and then mold me to fit all your plans?"

"What in the world are you talking about?" His arm swept wide. "We were dancing! Kissing! We made love, and don't say you didn't feel it too because I was there! I'm asking you to stay this time! How much clearer can it be?"

"That's the problem. It's crystal clear!" Oh, why couldn't he have just remained asleep then, so they didn't end everything with an argument?

Jason heaved a sigh. "You were going along just fine, to my recollection," he snapped back.

Her chin flattened. "That's a low blow."

"I'm a little frustrated here. All of a sudden I'm under attack and I'm not sure why."

"So what happens after tomorrow?"

"I don't know."

She laughed bitterly. "Sure you do, Jason. Just say it. What's the plan?"

His eyes darkened, wary. He couldn't escape the thought that he was somehow walking into a trap. But he couldn't put his finger on it. She was right, he did have a plan. He'd been thinking about their situation a lot lately, so of course he'd come up with a scenario or two.

"Well, since you're job's already on the line, you could quit before they have the chance to fire you...and stay here. Kim and Sara would love having you around more. We could take the time to see where this is going... I never stopped loving you Molly, you know that."

"And then?"

Her voice was dangerously low and his lips thinned in response. She could tell he sensed the trap she was setting but wasn't sure where it was. His response had been so close to her own plans it was eerie...and terrifying. Yet he still couldn't see what it was she needed from him.

"And then I suppose our relationship will go to the next level. I never told you this but I kept the..."

"Stop. Right. There."

He stopped at her dire command.

"You don't get it, do you?" She smoothed down her blouse and jeans, trying to wipe away any sense of the seduction she'd felt while in his arms. "Don't you see what you're doing? You're making me fit the mold of what *you* want. *Again.* Who would be making all the sacrifices here, Jason? Certainly not you. Your life will remain exactly as you've ordered it while mine gets turned topsy-turvy. You see what works for you and expect everyone else to see that too, and order their lives around yours."

"But you already said there are no ties back in Calgary."

"So what? It's my life. It might not be perfect, but it's what I've built for myself. Why is it any less important than yours?" She was defending a life that didn't really even exist anymore. But Jason had to understand. He knew nothing of her longing to reconnect with her sister and to start a new job, make a difference. And right now that wasn't the point at all.

He squared off now, growing angrier. "What is the big issue here? You know you want to be closer to Kim and Sara. You still have feelings for me; don't deny it. What is it that's holding you back?"

She stared into his eyes, and said with no ambiguity at all, "You."

His mouth opened and shut; for once he was completely speechless.

"You are the one holding us back. Because you can't even see why. I loved you then and I'll admit my feelings for you were never resolved, but you want exactly the same thing now you did then. You have everything planned out for me, perfectly ordered like some cutter life that suits you. But that's not me, Jason, and you've never been able to see beyond that."

"What are you talking about? It's always been you, Molly." He stared at her. His hands threaded through his hair in frustration while she took two steps backward. "Is there anything so wrong with wanting to be with you? To love you? To want a family with you?"

"But it's all on *your* terms!" she shouted back at him. Why couldn't he see that?

"I don't have terms. All I know is what makes sense. And from where I'm standing, it's simple."

"Nothing is simple, not with you."

"Don't you get it? I tried over the years to move on. God knows I tried." He let out a bitter laugh, dropped his hands. "But it never worked. Ask Kim."

Molly's eyes narrowed, her heart grew heavy with dread and her words were iron-lined velvet. "Ask my sister what?"

His eyes blanked as he scrambled for words. "It's just that..." He stopped, floundering.

"What exactly is there between you two, anyway?" Molly's stomach lurched painfully. In the flash of a few seconds, she saw his face, pale with worry over Kim, Kim's reaction to his name, the way he was with Sara... There was more. More they hadn't told her, and more she needed to know *right now* before she went any further.

"Nothing. Friends, I swear it."

But his lips thinned and his eyes were evading, caught in a trap of his own making.

"But there was, wasn't there."

"A long time ago," he admitted. "She was alone. I was helping her out... I thought that if we could try it, maybe it would work out... I could move on and she'd...you know."

Molly looked away, embarrassed. Dear Lord. What had she done? Never in a million years had she thought Jason was the kind of man to sleep with two sisters. She had to know for sure. At this point there was nothing more to lose...

"Yeah. I know." Molly couldn't keep the bitterness out of her voice. "So did you sleep with her, too?"

"What?"

"Close your mouth. You can't be that surprised. I'm asking if you slept with my sister, then slept with me."

"Molly, for God's sake!" His eyes widened as he stared, incredulous. "Do you really think I'd do that?"

"I don't know, Jason. I just don't."

"Well, let me enlighten you. I never slept with Kim. *Never.* We were both alone and lonely. We thought we might try something more. Kim's a special woman…so strong. She's been through so much. I would never trifle with her feelings unless we were sure."

Molly stared at her toes as he continued. "But once we kissed, I knew…"

"Just don't." She cut him off, held up a hand. "I don't want to hear the details about you kissing my sister."

"But Molly, it wasn't…"

She raised her head, her eyes burning fiercely at him. "Don't. The fact that this happened and neither of you told me…" She remembered asking Kim about it point-blank and receiving nothing but an evasive answer. "Even when I asked, Kim denied it." Her voice rose as she let the anger in. "You should have told me before I made a fool of myself."

And before she'd hurt her sister. The only family she had. She'd just begun making amends. And now instead of closure so Jason and Kim could move on, all she'd done was come in and muddle things even further. She did know how things were between Jason and Kim. From the first moment she'd seen them together, they'd seemed to fit in a way she didn't. Jason was good for Kim, and she would give him the family he wanted. It had been foolish of her to get in the way. Foolish of her to get involved with him at all.

She'd been the one to walk away all those years ago. Kim deserved someone like Jason who wanted the same things she did. Now Molly and Jason had slept together and she had that on her conscience as well.

"And why would it matter anyway? You don't want me. You don't want the life I have here." His voice intruded, harsh and condemning.

That was what he thought, because that was what she'd wanted him to think. He couldn't know how far it was from the truth.

"And what would Kim think if she knew you and I had sex all over that throw blanket?" She eyed him squarely, daring him to wither with guilt beneath her stare.

He had the grace to blush, but shoved his hands into his pockets, shrugging with a nonchalance she thought unbelievable. "She'd probably wonder what the hell I was thinking, setting myself up for hurt again."

Molly sagged. She was hurt and humiliated, but she was too tired to be angry anymore. Three weeks of being on a constant emotional rollercoaster finally took their toll and she gave up.

"Maybe I'll ask her," she said sadly. "Before I leave in the morning." She knew she wouldn't. She'd never reveal to her sister what had just happened with Jason. She'd hurt Kim enough.

"Molly." His voice gentled, but she couldn't look up through the sudden prick of tears she felt when he said her name in *exactly that way*.

"I've got to go," she said weakly. Deep down, she knew she was planning on leaving Calgary, leaving her job and looking for one that was more rewarding. But her personal life was shambles. She'd be somewhere closer to Kim, but she wasn't sure anymore that Fredericton was it. Being this close to Jason... It wouldn't work. If he finally moved on from her with her sister, it would be a painful death every time she saw them together until her heart simply withered away into nothingness. There was simply too much to deal with. And she'd dealt with it for long enough.

"So where does that leave us?" he asked hoarsely, perching on the edge of the sofa as their argument evaporated in the tiny shadows cast by what was left of the fire. His cheeks sagged in the dim light.

Molly saw his expression and felt the overwhelming sadness of *the end*. This was the end of the line for them. Things would never be the same. Only now she would say goodbye like she hadn't before.

"We're certainly not the same as we were three weeks ago," she replied. "We were full of anger and questions and resentment. I think we needed to talk, to get things out in the open. And to realize that we'd never really moved on. But I came here tonight to say that goodbye, Jason. And I'm more sure than ever that it is the right thing to do."

"I'm not."

She smiled sadly at his determined tone. "You're just mad that you're not getting your own way. In the end, you'll realize that this is what's right."

She walked over to where he was sitting and placed a soft hand on his face. His eyes closed at her touch and she knew despite her words, she was going to have to try to get over him all over again. Good luck with that.

"It's better this way," she said gently. "We'd end up hating each other. We're better off letting it go without anger and resentment eating away at us, spoiling whatever's left. You deserve the life that you want. With someone who wants the same things." *Like Kim,* she thought, but didn't say.

"Don't," he warned. "Don't get all philosophical on me. You're leaving. You'd better get back and get packed."

She withdrew as if he'd slapped her. She'd tried to make this as amicable as possible, but the intensity of their feelings stood in the way of it. He was very clear on what he wanted now—his own way again. It should have made the final decision easier, but right now all she could feel was empty hurt.

"Thank you for all you've done, for me and for my family," she whispered, her throat clogging with tears. "And Jason?"

He lifted his head, but his eyes were closed off and icy-cold.

"I'm sorry," she choked out, then spun from the room. She fumbled with her boots and jacket in her haste to get out the door. Once it was shut behind her she ran for home, sobbing all the way.

CHAPTER TEN

Kim was still up and sitting in the kitchen having a cup of tea when Molly got home. Molly was in no mood to talk, about anything. She took the stairs two at a time, pulled out her suitcase and started packing.

When her sister knocked on the closed door, she sighed. "What?"

"Are you okay?"

Molly felt the tears start again and knew she could not face Kim right now. Things were too raw, the wounds too open. She swallowed the huge ball of emotion in her throat and tried a more chipper, "I'm fine, just packing."

A pause.

"Do you want some help?"

Molly's hands paused holding a shirt. They were sisters, but despite everything, they'd never been confidantes. When would that have happened? Molly hadn't even been around for the past several years. She couldn't open up to her sister now. Especially not with how she felt about Jason or, more importantly, how she felt about *Kim and Jason*. How she felt knowing something was between them.

She wandered closer to the door, placed a hand on it. "Would you mind if I said I need some time alone?"

Kim's voice was close, just on the other side of the wood. "Not at all." Another pause. "But...Molly, if you need anything, come get me."

Molly's eyes stung again. Dammit. Kim deserved happiness. She gave and gave of herself, rarely getting anything in return. Now that Molly was getting out of the way, now that she and Jason had finally dealt with their own breakup, maybe something would happen so they both would be happy.

And that should make her happy. But it didn't, and she felt small and petty knowing she couldn't put their future happiness ahead of her own.

Kim moved on down the hall and Molly absently laid the shirt in the case and sat on the edge of the bed, dazed.

How could she muster up happiness, while her body still hummed from making love to him earlier?

She still loved him. But he wasn't going to sacrifice anything for her, and maybe she was wrong for asking him to. He wanted home and family and the life he had here. If ever two people had the same goals and aspirations in life, it was Jason and Kim. Molly would go back to Calgary and get out of the way. She was leaving the firm, of that she was sure. But returning here no longer seemed an option. Not unless she was into self-torture, and she wasn't. The past few weeks had taught her that. They had assured her that sometimes love, sometimes passion weren't enough. Kim had learned that long ago—with Sara's father.

It all made sense...except to Molly's heart. And what her heart knew was that she'd never love another man as she loved him. As she packed the last of her things and zipped up the bag, tears ran down her cheeks, hot and devastating. Still clothed and completely worn out, she crawled under the comforter and cried herself to sleep.

The following morning was somber and tinged with sadness. Molly had tried to camouflage her swollen eyes and rough cheeks with makeup, but it hadn't worked very well. Sara picked at her cereal, her usual bubbly chatter absent. Kim made a second pot of coffee and Molly checked her watch. Eight forty-five. She had a little over an hour to make sure she had everything and say goodbye. Once things got settled, once she knew exactly what she was doing, she'd tell Kim her plans. But she didn't want to say anything now, not when so much was undecided.

Time was too short. And it was too long. In some ways, she'd be much happier making it quick and painless and leaving right now.

"Maybe Sara and I can make a trip out this summer," Kim offered. Her post-accident paleness was gone but unmistakable misery lined her face.

"I'd like that," Molly replied, even though she doubted she'd still be in Calgary by summer. "We could go to the zoo and the dinosaur museum."

Fun, hah. It sounded lackluster and they both knew it.

"You talked to Jason?"

Molly took a few moments to add sugar and cream to her coffee. She couldn't exactly hide her face, so smiled ruefully and pointed to her eyes. "Obviously."

It wasn't in her to be mad at Kim for not telling her about kissing Jason. Molly had realized last night that with everything that had been dealt with over the past few weeks, she wasn't even sure how that conversation could have taken place. The fact of the matter was that six years ago she'd left them both, and Kim was single and next door. It wasn't fair of Molly to judge. In fact, what hurt the most was knowing that Kim would be better for him than she would. That Kim would make him happy in a way that Molly never had. All it would take was her getting out of the way so they could get on with it.

"Uncle Jason loves you," Sara piped up, swirling her spoon in the milk in the bottom of her bowl.

"Sara!"

The girl looked up at her mother, eyes wide and innocent. "Well, he does. 'Cause he was kissing her the way you said people kiss when they love each other."

Kim's cheeks flamed brilliant red, as did Molly's. She didn't intend for Kim to find out exactly what had happened at Jason's last night, and that carried its own level of guilt.

"Honey, why don't you make sure your hair and teeth are brushed? I'll be up in a minute."

Sara slid off her chair and headed for the stairs, but turned at the last minute. "I wish you could stay, Aunt Molly. You're fun."

Molly couldn't help but choke out a laugh. Had it only been a few short weeks ago when she'd been at her wits end trying to care for Sara? Her feelings for her niece now went far beyond any familial obligation. Sara would be the bright spot when she returned, either for a visit or if Molly decided to come back east to stay.

When she was gone, Kim said quietly, "What kiss?"

Molly sighed. "The day we went sledding. Sara and I pulled a trick on him, and one thing led to another... I'm sorry Sara saw it, though. We should have been more discreet..."

"You guys are idiots."

Molly's cheeks flushed brighter. "Thanks a lot."

Kim stood up and took her mug to the sink, but Molly could tell but the restless way she moved that she was more than a little annoyed.

"You guys love each other. You always have." Kim put the mug on the counter and spun, pinning her sister with an accusing stare. "Yet you're both so stubborn!"

"You don't understand."

"Then explain it to me. Explain how you can turn your back on a man who loves you so much, one that you love! One who wants to marry you and give you children and a home?"

Molly kept her voice level. "That's your dream, Kim, and I'm sorry it didn't work out for you. Maybe now...with me out of the way..." she started to stammer and her cheeks flushed deeply. How in the world could she find a graceful way to say this? "You are the kind of woman Jason wants. What he needs. It's better if I go now."

"What in the world are you talking about?" Kim folded her arms and stared at Molly.

"I know about you and Jason."

"What about us?"

"About...about the kiss. But it's more than that. I've seen how you are together. He cares for you so much, and I'm sorry I've stood in the way of that. Maybe now—"

"You really are crazy." Kim left her spot and took the chair next to Molly. "You seriously think there's anything between Jason and me?"

"He told me about kissing you. I saw his face when he told me about your accident. And then the day you came home...when he said the place had never been the same without you. It all adds up, don't you see?"

Kim smiled gently. "I can see it adds up *for you.*"

"Jason's always wanted a home here, and his business, and a family of his own. He wants all the things that you want. But he's never felt free to move on, and that's my fault for letting things end so badly."

"You're right, of course."

Molly's eyes widened as Kim smiled fondly.

"We do want the same things. But not with each other. Didn't Jason tell you about the kiss?"

"He told me you'd kissed. That's all."

"He helped me one night, and when he left he surprised the hell out of me." Kim chuckled lightly. "The kiss was a flop. I wasn't you. And I knew it. The convenience of it wasn't enough. I love Jason as a brother and best friend. I was still half in love with Sara's father and he was still in love with you."

Kim blushed but pursued. "We agreed not to tell you. We didn't want to cause problems over something that doesn't even matter anymore."

And if nothing had really happened.... She could even understand why they hadn't told her. Sure, she'd gone ballistic on Jason, but there was too much between them. Small things took on giant proportions where they were concerned.

"So you're not in love with him?"

"Of course not. We just...get each other."

Molly's brow furrowed. "But that's what I mean. You're just much better suited."

"Love doesn't have to have a reason, Mol." Kim reached out and took Molly's hand. "Are you seriously going to sit there and tell me you don't love Jason Elliot?"

Ah, the moment of truth. She was leaving, what did it matter now if she confessed all to her sister?

"Of course not. I still love him. I always have. But the reasons why I left six years ago haven't changed. At all."

Kim's shoulders slumped. "Neither one of you has ever been able to compromise."

Molly stood, pushing her chair in to the table. She was so tired of no one getting this!

"That's where you're wrong. I'd compromise in a second. I would have then, too. But Jason doesn't leave any room for compromise. Would you want us to get married, have a kid or two and end up resenting each other? What kind of life would that be? You have a daughter. Would you want that for her?"

Kim looked away and Molly felt a brief stab of guilt. Kim didn't even know where the lowlife was now. Sara had never even met her father. Probably never would.

"You know I wouldn't want that for either of you."

"Neither do I. I was wrong to leave things as I did. I know that. I admitted it to Jason, even. I didn't want to leave things so badly this time. I went over to talk to him last night, but I realized nothing has changed with him. He still wants me to fit into his plans for a perfect life. And that's why I'm leaving." Tears threatened again. "I'm not leaving because I'm some cold-hearted career woman. I've been hurt enough, surely you can see that much."

Kim came forward and wrapped her arms around her sister. "I'm sorry, Mol," she whispered. "I just got used to having you back. Now you're leaving again, and I want you to stay. You're all the family I have."

Molly sniffled loudly. "I know, and I'm sorry I've been selfish and stayed away so long. I wasn't going to tell you this but... I'm quitting my job. I want to come home. Maybe not here—it'd be too awkward—but closer. Closer to you and Sara."

"And closer to Jason."

"That's over. We ended everything last night."

Kim tipped up Molly's chin. "He doesn't know you're coming back."

Molly shook her head. "No. He did exactly the same thing, Kim. Presented me with this whole plan of how my life would go for the next few years. Didn't even ask what I wanted. I can't do it."

Kim hugged her again. "I know."

They pulled apart, smiling self-consciously. Not in years had they shown so much affection, been as honest with each other.

"There's more to life than climbing the corporate ladder. I think I'm ready to see that now. That and whatever else life has to offer."

"My big sister is growing up," Kim quipped, breaking the tension and making them both laugh.

"I've gotta go," Molly said sadly. "I need to return my rental and get checked in. You know the drill."

"You're sure you don't want us to come with you?"

"I'm sure. I said my goodbyes to Jason last night, and I want to get on that plane without crying. If you and Sara are there, I'll lose it for sure. But I'll call you and let you know my plans as soon as I can."

Sara came back downstairs, blonde curls brushed prettily and flashing her newly cleaned teeth. "See, Aunt Molly? I did it like you showed me."

Molly smiled. "That's right, sweet thing." Her voice broke a bit as she used one of Jason's pet names for her niece. "Listen, I've got to go now. But you be a good girl for your mom, okay?" She knelt down and hugged Sara's warm body, filling with bittersweet joy as the little arms squeezed around her neck. "I promise it won't be so long before I see you again." She kissed the baby-soft cheek pressed so close to her own.

"I'll miss you."

"Oh, I'll miss you, too. More than you'll know. Thanks for being such a good girl for me while Mom was in the hospital."

Molly put on her overcoat, the one she'd worn when she'd come home, and twisted the scarf around her neck.

"Okay. Just a *'til next time*, then. I'll call you when I get in to Calgary."

Kim stayed where she was, keeping the moment as light as they possibly could. "Thank you, for everything. We couldn't have managed without you."

"Anytime," Molly answered and, with a false smile, grabbed her suitcase and lugged it through the door to the waiting car.

Jason poured another cup of coffee from the office pot, grimacing at how thick and black the brew seemed to be today. He needed it, though. He'd stayed up most of the previous night, replaying his goodbye to Molly.

Maybe he should have fought more, tried harder. But he hadn't, because somewhere in the back of his mind he'd known she was right, and it had cut his argument off at the knees. Now he was in the middle of his work day, keeping appointments and doing what he did best...healing. Although why he was so competent healing animals but not dealing with his own problems, he didn't understand.

Pouring the remainder of his caffeine sludge down the sink, he went to his next appointment. Work had always been his panacea, the one thing that grounded him, and he knew he'd been right to follow his dream of becoming a vet. Normally, his troubles evaporated when he was here at the clinic he'd started on his own. But now, when his mind should be on work, he couldn't escape the sad look in Molly's eyes last night. She hadn't been angry, just accepting. Knowing exactly what he would say because he'd been thinking the same way he had when he'd proposed all those years ago.

He wanted a family, a wife and a couple of kids running around. A haven to come home to at the end of the day. It was what he'd always wanted, ever since his brother had died and his parents had changed.

They loved him, he knew. And they'd stayed together through their grief, yet things had never been the same after Jonathan died, and more than anything Jason had wanted to recapture that familial happiness that had existed before the tragedy.

He knew that, acknowledged it. Stripping off his latex gloves, he sighed. But what he hadn't understood, not really, was that he had been so single-mindedly focused on having the perfect family that he'd tried to command every single detail. He'd organized their life according to his vision, down to the most trivial thing, and spanning several years. Where they would live. Where they would work. When they'd have babies, for Pete's sake! He had been so afraid of losing his chance at happiness and family that he'd taken control. He'd wanted that family only with the girl, then woman, he'd fallen in love with. And he'd been afraid of losing her, so he'd tried to order everything and make her fit the mold.

He'd even seduced her last night, thinking that if he could get her to admit that she wanted him, if he could make love to her and remind her of all they'd had, she'd come around.

She had been different. More. Her body more lush, curved. It hadn't been just sex and she hadn't been a girl in love with a boy. She'd been all woman. No one since had fired his blood the way she had. No woman ever filled him with super-human strength with a simple touch or smile. But she did. And he'd blown it when he'd mentioned Kim.

Backtracking hadn't been enough. She'd set the trap and he'd walked right into it. And opened his big fat mouth.

But you couldn't control life and you sure as hell couldn't control other people. Especially someone as strong and determined as Molly. And it had been his fear of losing that had caused him to lose her anyway.

"Boss? You okay?"

Jason turned at the sound of one of the office assistants.

"Sure. Why?"

"Because I told you that we're low on amoxicillin and you said to take a message."

He stared. "Sorry, Bess. I'm a little preoccupied. We should have more stock with the next drug order."

"Okay." She smiled a little quizzically at him. "I'll just get back to work."

Jason went downstairs, locked himself in the bathroom and leaned over the sink. He ran some cold water and splashed his face, looking in the mirror at his drawn eyes and grim lips. Who was he kidding? He was miserable. He'd blown it for the second time. All the planning to show Molly what she had given up had done nothing but blow up in his face. Instead, he'd told her about kissing Kim. Talk about your awkward situations. But in the end, he knew she was leaving because he hadn't been able to admit he had something to learn, too.

And that was going to change, starting right now.

When she'd asked him last night about what he envisioned, he'd sensed a trap but had gone ahead with what he'd allowed himself to fantasize about. His house, no longer empty but ringing with her laughter. Sleeping beside her at night, hearing her even breathing, the warmth of her body seeping into his. He'd pictured her rounded with pregnancy and glowing, beautiful. Had seen her years in the future, a handful of kids around her as she packed school lunches and checked homework, soothed tears and celebrated successes.

That's what he'd wanted. But again, he hadn't asked what she wanted. He'd let her go, never attempted to connect with her again because he had always been sure she'd been the one in the wrong. Finally, he was beginning to see that her dreams were every bit as important as his. And he hadn't even asked her what hers were! He'd accused her of being self-absorbed when he'd been the one guilty of that transgression.

What did he have, really? Besides an empty house and a sixty-hour work week? He loved his work, yes, but his personal life? Shambles.

If the past three weeks had accomplished nothing else, they had made him realize one thing. He hadn't been living, not really. He'd been going through the motions, salving his need for family with the girl next door and her daughter, avoiding getting out there and experiencing life. The few times he'd attempted relationships, they'd fallen flat, never lasting very long. In the last three weeks, whether he and Molly had been fighting, not speaking or kissing, the end result had been the same. Being with Molly again had made him feel more *alive* than he'd felt in years.

He'd learned there was more than one way to be happy.

And right now she was getting on an airplane and flying away from him. *Again. And for good.*

He opened the bathroom door and went back upstairs, looking around with new eyes. Yes, he'd built a lucrative business, but he could do that anywhere. He couldn't imagine living in a world where he didn't do what he loved, but he couldn't imagine doing what he loved without Molly by his side either. Without her, everything seemed pointless, and he knew now that if he let her get away a second time he would never forgive himself.

His employees bustled around, doing their jobs, but now it didn't seem as meaningful to him. Not without her.

He looked at the clock on the wall. She was probably already gone, he realized. Still, he knew that if he didn't at least try, he'd regret it every single day of his life. If he had to, he'd buy a ticket to Calgary and go after her himself.

He stripped off his lab coat, hung it on a hook and grabbed his jacket. "Tell Mark I had to go out, and I'm sorry. Reschedule if you can. I won't be back today."

"But Dr. Elliot..."

But he was already out the door and jogging toward the truck. It was a five-minute drive to the airport. Maybe he wasn't too late. But he had to make a stop first.

As Jason skidded into the parking lot, he saw an airplane taking off, nose up, heading into the low cloud cover. He swung into the first empty space he saw and didn't even bother with change for the meter. If she was gone, there was only one thing to do—go after her.

&x&

"Flight eight-seven-four-three to Toronto is now boarding. All passengers should now proceed through security to the gate."

Molly looked at her watch. Well, at least they were going to board at the revised scheduled time. They should have been boarding a half hour ago, but she'd been left sitting in the lounge, drinking stale coffee while the crews de-iced the plane. Oh well...it would make her layover in Toronto shorter, she supposed. Finally, now, it seemed she could get on board and get back to disassembling what was left of her life.

And oh, how very dull that sounded.

She had some major changes to make. And first on her list was looking for a new job or possibly setting up her own practice. Someplace where she could feel useful and make a difference. She didn't quite know where that was, but she knew for sure it wasn't in her drab brown downtown office. Surely, somewhere closer to home, someone had need of a savvy corporate attorney.

She stood up and put the strap of her carry-on luggage over her shoulder, careful not to spill what was left of her coffee. She had her boarding pass in hand and was making her way to the security line when she heard it.

"Molly!"

She shook her head. She was just imagining things, her mind creating fanciful illusions. Leaving Jason last night had been the hardest thing she'd ever done...even harder than it had been six years ago. She could have gone through the metal detector sooner, into the secure area, but had stayed in the cafeteria simply because somewhere deep inside, a small part of her had hoped he'd come. This was simply her longing for him manifesting itself and she disregarded it.

"Molly!"

There was no mistaking it this time. Turning completely around, she saw Jason jogging down the hall toward her, his jaw set determinedly. *Don't give in,* she chanted to herself. *Just because he's here doesn't mean he's right.*

He stopped in front of her and she looked up, struggling to keep her face neutral while the rest of her traitorous body rejoiced at seeing him. His cheeks were ruddy from cold and hurrying, his hair disheveled as if he'd run his fingers through it a million times. To Molly, knowing it was the last time she'd see a long time, he'd never looked more alluring.

"What are you doing here, Jason? We said our goodbyes last night."

He stopped her progress in line with a hand on her arm. "*You* said goodbye. I didn't."

She looked around—several passengers were watching curiously, hearing every word. "They've just called boarding. We were delayed. I have to go."

"Just...wait." He tugged on her arm, pulling her out of line and she followed simply so the rest of the people couldn't hear what he was saying.

She searched for the words to say what she knew had to be said. "I've got to go, Jason. I tried to make you see that last night." *Steady,* she reminded herself.

"I know you did and you were right. Now it's my turn to have my say."

"I was right?"

He let go of her arm and to her surprise, laughed. "I know, I didn't think I could admit it either." He smoothed a hand over her cheek. "Yes, Molly, you were right. About everything.

"You were right about what happened six years ago. I did have this whole picture of our lives together, and I couldn't see that it wasn't what you wanted. When you left, I was convinced that you'd left *me.* But you didn't, did you?"

"No," she murmured. "I ran from your plan, but not from you. I loved you."

He paused, letting that confession swirl around them both, the importance of that beautiful truth finally sinking in as she finally said the words.

"I couldn't see that. All I could see was my dream of a home and family with you wasn't what you wanted, and I wasn't willing to compromise. I've never gotten over you, don't you see? Then you came back and I wanted to hate you. I could see how lonely my life had become and I wanted to blame you. It worked for a while, too. Until that day we went sledding." He reached down and took her hands in his. "I was scared, and then I was angry, and then I realized I'd never stopped loving you. I didn't know what to do with that."

"There's nothing *to* do with that. You still want me to fall in line with some master plan of yours and I just can't." Even though she had talked to Kim, she couldn't resist saying, "Kim is so much more what you want out of life."

"How could she be what I want when I'm not in love with her?"

That stopped her, and she swallowed. Now she'd heard it from both sides.

"I can't," she finally managed to say. "It would end up hurting us both far more than if we walk away friends now. Please," she implored him. "Let me do that. Let me walk away as your friend." *And let me come back and be friends.*

"I can't do that. Not after loving you last night. Not after remembering everything."

She pulled her hands away from his and adjusted her carry on. "I've got to go."

The female voice came over the intercom and announced final boarding for the flight. Molly took the first steps away from him. Her heart was heavy as she realized she was walking away from him, from them, honest and truly for good. Even when she knew she was doing the right thing, it felt very wrong.

"Don't get on that plane," he said loudly, causing heads to turn in his direction. When Molly spun tears were in her eyes, her lips pursed up in frustration.

"Why are you doing this to me?" she hissed, her eyes shooting daggers at him. "Just let me go!"

"Never again," he answered, shaking his head. "It's not the same this time, Molly. Let me show you."

"Show me what?"

"That you're it for me."

The passengers had stopped moving; even the security guards stood watching the scene instead of putting bags through the metal detector. For Molly they ceased to exist. She only saw Jason's dark eyes focused on hers, found herself gazing back, longing for him to say the right words this time. She cursed the hope that fluttered in her chest. She hadn't let herself hope.

"That's never been the issue," she choked.

"Then I'll prove it. I'll put the house up for sale and let Mark buy out my share of the clinic. I can start over again, easily. It doesn't matter where. I can come to Calgary and be with you, or we can go somewhere new and start over together. Whatever you want."

He didn't mean it. He couldn't. Jason Elliot, Mr. Five Year Plan, wasn't actually breaking ties and taking unknown chances, was he? She wanted to believe him. She'd never wanted anything more than to believe that he could trust her with their future. But a tiny part of her still nagged that it was too good to be true. She kept the distance between them, still wary.

"You're just saying that to get me to agree."

He started walking slowly toward her. "You're right. I am. Because right now there's nothing that matters half as much as being able to love you for the rest of my life. I'll give it all up if you'll marry me this time, Molly."

He reached her and she had to tilt up her head to look into his eyes. He was serious. He was willing to give it all up to be with her. On her terms. Nothing ever could have meant more to her than the sacrifice he was willing to make to be with her. She swallowed, suddenly aware that her cheeks were wet with tears and that thirty-odd people were waiting with held breath for her answer. He hadn't known she'd been planning to come back all along...and he was willing to uproot his life to be with her! She sniffed, laughed, turned to the security personnel and said, "You'd better get these people through. I won't be boarding."

A cheer went up through the crowd, voices laughing and hands clapping as she turned back to Jason, dropped her bag and wrapped her arms around his neck. "My answer's yes," she whispered, gasping when his arms lifted her feet clear of the floor and he kissed her, fully, jubilantly.

The crowd dispersed and he put her down. "I was so scared," he murmured, pressing his forehead to hers. "I was sure you'd say no, and I wasn't sure how I was going to manage without you. I thought after last night I didn't stand a chance."

"You mean it? We can start our life anywhere?"

He nodded. "It'll take some arranging with the house and business, but nothing a good lawyer can't handle." He winked at her and she grinned widely. He dipped into his coat pocket. "I have something for you."

Stepping away, he knelt down on the cold white tiled floor and opened the ring box with a stiff creak.

"This ring has waited six years to be on your finger. Don't make it—or me—wait any longer."

He took it out of the velvet and slipped it over the finger of the hand she held out. It was a perfect fit, even now.

He rose, still clasping her hand, turning the diamonds over with his fingers.

"Jason? You don't need a lawyer."

He stopped twirling and furrowed his eyebrows at her. "I don't?"

"You don't need legal counsel. You aren't going to sell the practice or the house. I love your house."

He stepped back, mouth gaping. Molly laughed, crossing her arms and pressing her fingers against her lips. He didn't realize. Didn't see that his willingness to sacrifice was all she'd really needed, and more than she thought he'd ever give.

"You don't get it, do you?"

"I thought you wanted to stay in Calgary, look after your career..." His brows furrowed in confusion.

"I know that's what you thought. But I can be a good lawyer anywhere. I love Calgary, but without you, it's..." She broke off, swallowing the tears that gathered in her throat. "What I wanted, you silly man, is the choice. To know that what I wanted was as important to you as what *you* wanted. A partnership, equal billing. To know that together we could find a compromise."

"And it took me six years to realize it."

"Better late than never."

"You really want to stay here?"

She smiled, feeling all the pieces click into place one by one. "I'd already decided to quit and leave Calgary. I don't belong far away, in a job that's cold and unfulfilling. I knew over a week ago that I wanted to come back and be closer to Kim and Sara and...you." She raised her hand and touched his jaw tenderly. "But I couldn't tell you. I needed you to offer that compromise so I could be sure. My heart broke last night when I thought I'd never get it. I was sure that if I got out of the way that there'd be room for you and Kim to be happy, because you both deserve that."

"That's ridiculous."

"I know that now. It's not up to me to try to dictate

your lives. It's not about plans and timetables. It's about hearts. And what hurt most is I knew without a doubt I'd never love anyone as much as I love you."

"I couldn't let you walk away again." He pressed his lips to her forehead and she closed her eyes.

"Excuse me for saying it, but I'm glad!" She laughed thickly.

"You're really coming home?"

"I was only going back to take care of business—like selling my condo and quitting my job. I'll stay with Kim until I get settled but...your house is big enough for both of us. Kim is next door—and it's high time I started being a sister and aunt, don't you think? I can't think of anything more perfect. I can hang out my shingle anywhere."

At a loss for words, Jason simply gathered her into his arms and closed his eyes in thankfulness.

"Let's go home," she whispered against his neck. "I've got the whole afternoon off, and this is one celebration that's long overdue."

EPILOGUE

Molly twisted the rings on her finger, trying to ease them off her hand. "Oh, this is ridiculous."

Jason laughed, picking up the hand and slipping the offending finger into his mouth. "I think it's cute," he said, nipping at the pink-colored fingernail.

With a snort, Molly ripped her hand away and turned the rings around until they finally slid over the knuckle. With a sigh, she put them on the coffee table and sank back into the cushions of the sofa.

"Mistake number two."

"Sitting down?"

"Sitting here," she complained ruefully. "You're going to need a block and tackle to get me up."

Jason leaned over, spreading his hand over the large mound of stomach protruding from the cushions. "It won't be long now. And you finished work today... We can finish decorating the nursery. Spend a few lazy mornings in bed....whatever you want, angel."

Leaving work had been hard. Molly had come to love her new job, working as legal counsel to a large non-profit for underprivileged kids. Knowing at the end of the day she was helping make a difference—it was much more fulfilling than endless land and gas leases, the power parties and pointless receptions.

But her due date was only a week away, her feet and hands were swollen, and she felt like a cow every time she moved. Sometimes she felt like all she needed was a damn bell around her neck.

She leaned ahead, huffing, and picked up the rings. "I didn't think I'd ever take these off." She pouted.

Jason reached behind her and unclasped her gold chain. "Here. We'll thread them on your chain and you can wear them close to your heart."

Molly stared down at the rings in her hand. The first, winking with diamonds, had waited six long years to sit on her finger, and she hated having to remove it, even for a few short weeks. The second was newer and even more precious because of the promises it held. "It doesn't seem right," she whispered, fingering the smaller band with three diamonds inset.

Jason strung the rings on the chain and re-hooked the clasp. Smiling, he pulled Molly backwards and wrapped his arms around her. "I'm glad you're so attached," he teased. "But as long as you don't get rid of *me,* we'll be just fine."

Her hand covered his, felt their baby move beneath their fingers. "Are you kidding? I waited far too long to have you to get rid of you now."

"So you did. But we got here, that's what matters."

The back door slammed; Molly angled her head to send her husband a knowing look. "We have company."

"Aunt Molly! Uncle Jason!"

How awkward Molly had felt the first time Sara had paired their names together well over a year ago. Now it was music to her ears.

"Hey, pumpkin," Molly called out. "Your mom with you?"

Sara bounded into the room, her blonde hair in bouncy ringlets and brown eyes sparkling with devilment. "She's coming. She's got brownies and fudge crackle ice cream.

Molly groaned in anticipation. "That's good. Junior hasn't had his chocolate fix today."

Jason reached down, jiggled the rings, mocking her. "Are you sure that's not what got you into this problem to begin with?"

Molly scowled darkly. Really. Jokes about weight gain were not a good idea right now.

"That would be water retention."

Kim's happy voice intruded and Molly sent her a thumbs up for the female solidarity. "Ah, the Estrogen Brigade has arrived. I heard you brought my daily fix. Help me up, will you?"

With Jason's hands pushing and Molly's gripping Kim's, she got to her feet.

With a popping sound.

Kim laughed, Jason raised his eyebrows, and Molly said, "Oops."

"Sara, honey, put the ice cream in the freezer. We've gotta go."

Molly smiled at Jason, unfazed by the contraction. They'd been happening all day, off and on, varying in intensity. "Could you get me some dry clothes, honey?"

"Now?"

"Right now." She put her hand on his, looking up into his awed, frightened eyes. "My water just broke. Besides, it's about time this show got on the road, don't you think?"

Jason's heart hit his throat.

His wife was standing there, calm as you please, in the middle of labor, and all he could do was stare at her dumbly.

The fact that she was laughing at him shook him out of his stupor. "Right. Bag. Hospital."

He was guiding her to the truck, Kim and Sara going to Kim's car to follow, when a contraction hit.

"Mmmm." She paused, pursing her lips.

"Mmmm?" He peered into her face.

"This one's a little stronger than the others."

Dear Lord. A contraction and all she could say was *Mmmm*? His wife was made of tough stuff.

"Let's go," she murmured, but he heard the underlying urgency in her voice and quickly got her in the truck and out the drive.

At the hospital she was taken immediately into a room for monitoring while he looked after paperwork. He tried to rush through admitting, hating every moment he had to spend away from her.

"Relax, Mr. Elliot." The clerk smiled up at him. "First babies take a while."

Easy for you to say. It wasn't her wife up there going through it. It wasn't *her* baby trying to come into the world.

When he returned, breathless from jogging up the stairs, Molly was sitting up on an angle, dressed in a hospital gown and chewing on ice chips from a clear plastic cup. A nurse went to the light switch and dimmed the lights in the room, creating a cozier atmosphere.

"Jason."

"I'm here."

He moved to her side, leaned over and kissed her forehead. "What can I do?" His fingers stroked her face and she relaxed.

"You're doing it."

Another contraction hit and she squeezed his hand.

"Good," said the nurse, checking her watch. "Three minutes. You're progressing nicely."

"Nicely. Great. I'm *so* glad I'm doing *nicely.*" She punctuated the sentence with a very ripe word.

The nurse looked at Jason, unfazed, a wry grin spreading on her face at Molly's acidic tone. "And we've hit transition. Not long now."

Until this moment, they'd almost been a family, but after tonight, there would be a baby, one that was part of both of them, a living testament to their love, their commitment. He thought he'd understood what that meant. There'd been the joy and fear of discovering Molly was pregnant. The knowing that he was going to be completely responsible for another life. There was that first heartbeat in the doctor's office, the first movement beneath his hand, the beautiful rounding of her as their baby grew. But nothing had made him realize how *big* this was, how magnificent and humbling, until he sat beside her, seeing her labor to deliver their son or daughter.

When their daughter, Alyssa Joy, came howling into the world, he hadn't known his heart was big enough to hold so much.

And he knew that if she'd asked, he would have made any sacrifice to be with her. Because together they *were* a family.

"Thank you," Molly whispered, dangerously close to tears.

He pressed his forehead to hers, damp with sweat.

"For what?"

"For giving me my happily ever after," she whispered.

He leaned back as the nurse placed a white wrapped bundle in Molly's arms. Two tiny pink lips sucked in and out, the tiny nearly-black eyes barely open, a scratch mark on one precious cheek.

"Now you see, that's where you've got it wrong." He smiled down, his eyes suspiciously damp as his lip quivered. "Because it's you who's given me what I always wanted."

"A family."

"Not just any family. Our family."

He kissed her then, with the baby between them. When their lips parted, he felt her smile against his mouth. "You have no idea, Elliot," she murmured. "This is just the beginning."

ABOUT THE AUTHOR

A busy wife and mother, **Donna Alward** believes hers is the best job in the world: a combination of stay-at-home mom and romance novelist.

An avid reader since childhood, Donna always made up her own stories. She completed her Arts Degree in English Literature in 1994, but it wasn't until 2001 that she penned her first full-length novel, and found herself hooked on writing romance. In 2006 she sold her first manuscript.

Donna loves being back on the East Coast of Canada after nearly twelve years in Alberta where her Harlequin career began, writing about cowboys and the west. She's a two-time winner of both the Bookseller's Best Award and the Colorado Award of Excellence, and a 2012 RITA finalist.

Donna loves to hear from readers.
You can contact her through her website at
www.donnaalward.com

Visit her Facebook page, or through her publishers.

Twitter: @DonnaAlward

**Keep reading for an excerpt from
THE GIRL MOST LIKELY**

THE GIRL MOST LIKELY

Katie wiped her sweating hands on her skirt, lifted her hand to knock on the dark wooden door and drew it back.

For the third time.

Why was she so afraid of seeing Richard Emerson again? They hadn't seen each other since high school. Surely they'd both grown up enough to leave unpleasantness behind. But the stakes were high now, at least for her. Richard was her last chance. She'd been standing before his office door for five full minutes and had yet to garner the courage to knock.

Before she could chicken out once more, she took a deep breath, rapped on the closed door three times and stepped back. She tugged at her navy skirt and matching jacket, hoping she looked professional. She needed him to take her seriously.

"Come in," a deep voice intoned, and she turned the knob. It was slippery in her palm and she exhaled, trying but failing to calm the nerves bouncing around in the pit of her stomach.

Stepping into the office, she saw him sitting in a seating area on the left. Richard, severe and imposing, was ensconced in a comfortable blue chair, files before him on a glass-topped, round table.

"I'll be right with you," he said without looking up.

She couldn't help but stare. Where was the lanky, nerdy boy she remembered? The man with the thick file before him wasn't the math geek she'd known all those years ago. His hair was rich and black with a hint of natural curl, and the sleeves of his dress shirt were rolled back to reveal strong forearms sprinkled with dark hair. Her eyes widened and pulse quickened at the sight of the man he'd become.

She forced herself to divert her attention to his office and was further discomfited by the startling neatness and the precision of organization. Honeyed hardwood covered the floors. A gigantic bookshelf covered one wall, each book spine lined up neatly. There was a beige file cabinet to one side, a smooth mahogany desk and a plush leather chair empty behind it. Everything was in an exact place. She wagered if she asked him where his extra staples were, he'd pull them out of a slot made specifically for that very purpose. All indications pointed to an orderly, analytical mind. In that way, she supposed, he hadn't changed a bit.

She heard the file close.

"Sorry about that, Miss..."

"Katie—"

He turned his head. "Buick," he finished, his lips curving up a bit in surprised recognition. "My God. It really is you. Dad said you might be dropping by."

"Yes, on business."

She wiped her hands on her skirt again, cursing inwardly at her awkwardness.

For a long moment, they stared at each other. She saw his eyes were the same deep brown, still fringed with thick lashes. They had always been his best feature. She counted back. Ten years ago, they'd graduated high school together. Ten years ago, he'd been the one with sweaty palms as he'd invited her to the prom. Ten years ago, she'd laughed in his face. Not that he'd helped his case any. He'd had scrawny arms and a pimply face and had generally been known as a complete nerd. Still, they'd had a few classes together and their parents were friends. He hadn't been bad to talk to. And he'd had big dreams. Katie'd admired that.

But he'd waited until three days before prom to ask her to go with him, and then he'd done it in public around all her friends. They'd never understand that Katie actually liked Nerdboy, as they called him. One of the girls—she couldn't even remember her name now—had made a snotty remark, and Katie had done something cruel—she'd laughed at him. Instantly, his cheeks had stained red and he'd shuffled away. She'd felt awful, but had never gotten up the courage to apologize. It hadn't been her finest moment.

Now the joke was on her. The man rising before her had certainly changed. His dark looks were now quite handsome. He'd lost his gawky teenage gangliness and his face was clear and tanned, smooth from his morning shave. He stood, his legs long and lean in the expensive fabric of his suit, while his shirt stretched taut across broad shoulders. In fact, besides the eyes and the shape of his mouth, it was almost like looking at a different person. He came forward, holding out a hand. She took it, hoping to God hers wasn't as clammy as she thought it must be.

She blushed, and he smiled again, the warmth not quite meeting his eyes as he withdrew his hand. "You have business. Care to sit?"

She stepped forward, her heels clicking like gunshots behind him on the hardwood floor of his office. It seemed to take forever to cross the expanse, evidence of how well he'd done for himself.

"Thanks. This is a beautiful office." *Way to go, Katie*, she thought. *Nice sparkling conversation you've got going.*

She took the chair opposite him, put down her portfolio and crossed her legs. Without thinking, she defensively crossed her arms.

"The perks of being the president," he remarked, closed the open file on the table and pushed it to one side. Folding his hands in his lap, he wasted no time. "What can I do for you today?"

Ouch. That sounded like a standard line if ever there was one. Looking up at him, she saw his face was impersonal and barely interested. How could she ever sell him on this idea?

"I'm starting a new business."

"What does that have to do with me?"

She bit down on her lip. "Well, unfortunately the financing has been...elusive."

"The banks turned you down." He cut straight to the chase and she winced.

"Yes." Oh, how it hurt to admit it. She'd tried everything, but no one wanted to take a chance on her idea or put the money behind it. She had no experience, few credentials—just a small dream and a desire to make it happen. Apparently, the promise to work hard didn't go very far in the business world.

She'd done her homework, and though the banks thought her too much of a risk, there was no doubt in her mind she could do this.

"Perhaps you'd better tell me about your venture, though I'm not sure how I can help. I assume it has nothing to do with land development?"

"No, it doesn't. But when I kept hitting brick walls, Dad suggested I try here." That had stung too. Both taking advice from her dad and resorting to nepotism. It was definitely humbling.

To avoid meeting his eyes, she gazed around his office once more. He was a land developer and it was obviously very lucrative. Katie smoothed her department-store skirt, terribly aware of how circumstances had changed. Richard—Ric—now held the power to reject her and her idea, and she wondered if he'd turn her down as simple revenge for how she'd treated him in the past. Until now, she'd done a good job of avoiding him. Sucking up to him and his bank balance was something that didn't appeal to her. If only she'd apologized all those years ago instead of leaving it be. But now their past was like another person in the room with them. She fought to get the words out.

"I want to open a restaurant."

He steepled his fingers and rested them on his lips. "I see."

"Not any restaurant. Something different."

"Everyone thinks their idea is different."

"Y-yes. I'm sure they do," she faltered. She had to convince him that her idea was innovative. And beyond that, profitable. But every time she looked at him, she only saw the hurt in his eyes that day when she'd laughed at him.

He crossed his ankle over his knee, the black trouser leg flawless. "Convince me."

Katie took a breath. Damn him for being completely in control, coolly implacable. She was sure her face was flushed, ruining any effect her careful application of makeup may have had. She uncrossed her arms and reached for her portfolio and the facts and figures she'd brought along to back her up.

"I want to open a healthy-choices type restaurant. Nothing upscale, in fact, it would cater mostly to the downtown lunch crowd. All of our selections would be based on sound nutrition. Whole grains, low in saturated fat, emphasis on vegetables and fruits, locally sourced and mostly organic. An alternative to fast food, if you will, but at the same time a step up. Something to grab on the run but also to sit down and enjoy."

"Do you seriously think it will fly?"

"Yes, I do," she replied, taking files out of her case. "In fact, I developed a bit of a survey about people's dietary habits, dining out habits and what sort of things they'd be interested in. I tabulated the results. It's clear. People are increasingly aware of their health and wanting to eat better, but they admit there seem to be few choices for eating out on a budget, and even fewer for eating out without overloading on starch and fats."

She handed him the survey but continued on as he looked at it, the words spilling out as nervous energy pushed her on.

"Several fast food chains carry salads now. And they're obviously popular, because they haven't pulled them from the market. They're slowly incorporating other healthier choices. The newest trend though, is not just healthy food but where and how it's grown. I'd like to get established now. What is it you say? Get in on the bottom floor?"

Richard looked up, met her eyes, and she felt a jolt. He had grown up well. Now he was rich. He'd always said he would be and people had pointed their fingers and laughed. He'd told her about it one afternoon at a brunch his parents had held. He'd remarked with some amazement that she was the first person who hadn't laughed at him.

Now here he was, president of his own company, mature, filled out and handsome. There was more to him than his physical appearance...it was power. It made for a potent combination.

"Katie? I asked if you had a sample menu."

She shook her head, pulled out a sheet and handed it over. "The breakfast menu is small, as you can see."

Ric scanned the menu but Katie continued, amazed he'd even asked to see one. "Egg-white omelets, low-fat muffins, multi-grain pancakes, oatmeal, cereals, fruit, Greek yogurt. I'd expect most of the morning traffic to be the coffee crowd, so we'd stock mostly muffins, tea and coffee. Our biggest rush would be at lunch. As you can see, we'd have two hot specials each day...for example, a vegetarian lasagna and perhaps chicken stir-fry with brown rice, that sort of thing."

He kept staring at the sheet and her stomach tumbled. Desperate to convince him, she plowed on.

"The sandwiches and wraps would be custom-made and served with a side of either one of three salads or a soup. Soup and a whole grain bun will also be a staple of the menu, as well as meal-sized salads. The nice thing about the sandwiches is that they are hot. Grilled chicken and mushroom. Lean steak and peppers. Roasted vegetables, for example. All may be made on a choice of whole-grain bread, wraps or pitas. No fried food of any sort. The dessert menu is also small. Fruit cup with dip. Fat-free chocolate cake with frozen yogurt. I'm still looking for dessert ideas." She looked up again, surprised his eyes hadn't glazed over.

"And dinner hour? Or does your plan include being closed over dinner?"

"The lunch selections will be available, but in addition we'll have a handful of dinner entrees. Grilled chicken breast, brown rice or baked sweet potato and steamed vegetables, salmon, sole, grass-fed beef. Marinara sauce with whole-wheat or gluten-free pasta. Fajitas. Depending on response we could, and should, adjust the menu accordingly." Katie took a breath as she finished.

He put down the menu and she got the sinking feeling she was going about this all wrong. *Business plan, business plan,* she chanted in her mind.

"Look, menus aside, the most important thing to realize is that there is a real hole in the market for this type of establishment. One of the biggest markets today is weight loss—food, programs, books, you name it. Come out with an eating establishment that carries great tasting food, healthy ingredients and the flexibility to fit it to a specific plan, and you've got a winner."

"And who would do the cooking?"

She paused, expecting some surprise at the least and, most likely, strict resistance. "Me."

"You?"

"Yes. I've worked in the food service industry for several years." She made it sound more than it was and felt a little niggle of guilt over fudging the details.

She should have known he'd persist. He quirked an eyebrow and she felt as if he saw right through that statement. "You've studied?"

"N-no," she stammered, "not exactly. I've, well, I've worked in several restaurants, either serving or in the kitchen."

He chuckled, leaning back in his chair. "Let me get this straight. You've got no money, no business experience, no chef's diploma to hang on the wall. You've got an idea. That's all. Does that sound like a strong investment to you?"

"Absolutely not," she admitted. "But what I do have is a strong desire to do this and I'm not afraid of hard work. I'm also not scared to learn."

"First of all, tell me why this is important to you." He leaned forward, elbows on his knees, waiting for her answer.

The question threw her. Not once in the meetings she'd held with bankers had they asked that particular question. They had only seen the bottom line—facts and figures. She'd faced the inquisition about work experience, and the answer had always been a resounding no. But Ric wanted to know the why?

"What do you mean?"

"I mean, why now, and why a restaurant? Why this particular kind of restaurant?"

She thought about her answer for a moment before answering. "I've worked in food service for a long time, but one thing always stuck with me. No real thought was put into nutritional content. The ingredients were always full of fat or made with white flour, deep fried or cooked in oil. When Dad had his heart attack, Mom and I started looking at healthier foods."

She leaned forward a bit, resting her hands on the edge of his desk. "You know my dad, Ric. Larger than life and going great guns. Seeing him lying in a hospital bed, frail and grey...it broke my heart. He came home with strict orders for a better diet and more physical activity. I was still living at home and Mom and I did some experimenting. She lost twenty pounds and Dad's color came back. The more I looked into it, I discovered there was a market for fast, healthy, economical food. That's when I realized it was something I could do."

"Do you realize how many entrepreneurs start businesses only to have them fail in the first two years?"

"The number fluctuates, but my research says around sixty percent. And for the food service industry, it's even higher."

Richard crossed his legs. "And you still want to go through with it?"

"I'll never know unless I try." Looking into his face, she would swear she saw a glimmer of admiration.

"Do you know what causes businesses to fail? Bad management. Poor marketing, location. Inadequate financing."

Katie put down the portfolio and started to feel defensive. She wasn't stupid, and she didn't like when people made her feel that way. She knew she could do this. She'd believed him when he'd said he'd be rich one day, and she could make it too.

"I know all that. But I believe in the idea and in myself. I've even found a space to lease. A little tea room off of Third Street. Tell me, Ric, how many people told you you'd fail when you started ELDC?"

"Plenty." For the first time, he smiled. "And I listened to every single one and learned from it."

He rose from his chair and wandered the office for a few moments. Katie forced herself to remain calm and seated. Finally, he spoke.

"If I were to finance you, there's still one sticking point for me. You'll never keep customers with poor quality. I think you should reconsider doing the cooking yourself and hire a professional."

"It would be foolish to spend the money on a cook's wages when I can do it myself. I'll already have to hire someone part-time anyway, because I don't plan to be there seven days a week *and* take care of the business end." A thought dawned on her and she ran with it. "I'll make you a deal. You pick a meal from this menu. I'll cook it for you tomorrow night. If you have any doubts about my cooking after that, I'll concede to hiring a chef."

"If you pass, I'll name my terms."

Katie's heart leaped. My God, he was actually considering backing her. All she had to do was cook him a fabulous, healthy meal. She forced herself to sit still while her body vibrated with hope.

He sat back in the blue chair again, retrieved the menu. After a few moments perusing it, he chose. "Chicken fettuccine, with spinach salad and the chocolate cake."

"It's a deal." Hastily, she took a note pad out of the portfolio and scribbled down her address. "Here's my address, show up at six. I guarantee you won't regret it, and we can iron out the details over dinner."

Richard looked down at the address. "You're very sure of yourself."

She stood, hoping her wobbly knees weren't obvious. She was glad he thought she was confident, because she felt anything but.

"Yes, I am."

"Then I'll see you tomorrow evening."

He stood and held out his hand, and she was acutely aware of how much he'd grown since high school. Even though she wore heels, he topped her by a good four inches. For a moment, she panicked. She felt like a teenager again, off-balance and insecure.

There was no way she could wipe her palm on her skirt now, and she hoped it wasn't damp when she clasped his. His fingers closed around hers firmly and her body was electrified by the simple touch.

"Goodbye, Katie."

"Um, yes. Goodbye, Richard."

She withdrew her hand, hurriedly retrieved her case and scuttled out the door, shutting it behind her.

In the elevator, she leaned back against the wall and took a few calming breaths. For the first time in several weeks, she felt hope. Hope that she'd actually get this venture off the ground.

Katie smiled widely at her reflection in the mirrored elevator wall. He hadn't said no. Now she was going to cook him a meal that would knock his socks off.

CPSIA information can be obtained at www.ICGtesting.com
Printed in the USA
LVOW06s1621160315

430763LV00005B/1492/P